Roy pitched directly into his brother

The X Bar X Boys
and the
Sagebrush Mystery

JAMES CODY FERRIS

A HAMLYN WESTERN

ANDREW DAKERS LIMITED
LONDON

Printed and bound in Great Britain by
Jarrold and Sons Ltd
Norwich

CONTENTS

"And the gun went flying across the room"

Chapter I

MYSTERIOUS VISITORS

A cloud of dust appeared on the horizon as two horsemen came across the vast prairie toward a cluster of ranch buildings.

"The Manley boys shore can ride, Gus!" drawled a young man in leather chaps and sombrero who was lounging by the front gate. "Look at 'em come in!"

His companion, similarly dressed, but older, removed a sliver of straw from his mouth. "Nick Looker, there ain't two better cowboys in the whole X Bar X outfit than Roy and Teddy," he stated.

In a few minutes two spirited horses thundered up to the gate and came to a pawing, bucking stop as their riders jumped to the ground.

"Hello, Nick! Good morning, Gus!" greeted one, a tall, brown-eyed boy with clear-cut features. "What's doing?"

"'Mornin', Roy. Gus and I was just wonderin' if you and Teddy was a-goin' to stop before you went through the bunk-house!" the cowboy laughed.

"Oh, come, now, Nick! You're not turning sissy, are you?" taunted the younger Manley brother, his blue eyes twinkling. "Why, we were just loafing along, weren't we, Roy?"

"I guess it depends on how hungry you are after riding fences since daybreak," replied Ted's brother. "Any speed would have seemed like loafing this morning!"

Laughing and joking, the lads and their cowboy friends strolled down to the corral, Roy leading his beloved pony Star and Teddy trailing along with Flash. The two thoroughbreds were the brothers' prized possessions.

"Well, it won't be long before round-up time, boys," Nick remarked. "Hope you're plannin' to be in on it."

"I'll tell a maverick!" exclaimed Roy. "Dad seems to think we have the best herd of cattle this year we've ever had!"

"And your dad knows cattle, too, don't you boys forget that!" declared Gus emphatically as the group reached the corral. As the elderly man swung open the gate, the ponies bounded in.

"I wouldn't trade Flash for her weight in diamonds," said Teddy, gazing fondly after his mount. "There just couldn't be a better one."

"Bossee Loy, Bossee Loy!" interrupted a high-pitched voice.

The squat figure of Sing Lung, the bunk-house cook, came hurrying toward them. His pigtail was flying and his face was twisted with worry.

"Someblody steal my money. Tlousand dollas!" he panted. "Takee flom closet!"

"Sing Lung! You must be fooling," said Roy.

The cook threw up his hands. "No foolee, Bossee Loy! Tlousand dollas, she gone!"

"Maybe one of the men has played a joke on him," said Teddy.

Roy scowled. "If you ask me, it's some joke to steal a thousand dollars from anybody. Maybe we'd better do a little sleuthing."

At length the boys were able to calm the upset

Chinaman with the promise that after breakfast they would try to locate the missing money.

"By the way, Ted, I wrote to Ed Bartlett last week," the older Manley boy remarked as the brothers proceeded toward the ranch-house. "Told him all about ranch life and invited him to visit us any time he can come."

"Ed's a fine fellow. Let's hope he can make it," Teddy said, referring to a boy who had been one of their chums at Hopper Boarding School near Denver.

"Better get your friend here in time to get him warmed up before the round-up!" Nick chimed in.

This young cowboy had grown up on the Manley ranch and was greatly attached to the boys, whom he had taught to ride. Now they knew almost as much as their instructor. Nick was always interested in teaching their friends and guests something of cowboy lore.

"You bet we'll get Ed here if we can," Teddy agreed. "Coming into the house with us?" The younger Manley boy pulled open the kitchen door of the rambling ranch-house and stood aside with a mock bow. "I'm sure Norine is in!"

The cowboy reddened. "I—I got some work to do, boys. See y'all later." He hurried off just as Norine Moore, plump and pretty, came to the door.

"Well, if you ain't two of the dustiest, mussed-up people I ever laid eyes on. I suppose you want some breakfast just that way!" exclaimed the girl in pretended seriousness.

"Hello, Norine!" Roy greeted her. "You're right about our wanting breakfast, but I guess we're not so dusty and mussed up as you say."

"Well, I guess I'll have to give you something to eat

even if it's only a few flapjacks and sausage," she said breezily.

"Suits me!" declared Roy. "Never tasted any that were better than the ones you make, Norine!"

The girl turned crimson. "Now, Roy, stop that nonsense!" she giggled. "Go on in the dining-room. Your folks are just about through eating."

Teddy smiled to himself as he caught sight of Nick lurking outside the kitchen door, waiting for the boys to leave. The handsome cowboy's romance with Norine was one of the subjects of gossip on the ranch, so the young man was the object of much good-natured banter among the men.

As the boys entered the dining-room, they found Mr. and Mrs. Manley and Belle Ada, their young sister, at the table. They had just finished eating.

"Good morning, boys!" boomed out Bardwell Manley from behind his pipe. "'Bout time you showed up. How's the fence?"

"Everything's fine, Dad," Roy reported. "Some of the wire was sagging a little down at Crooked Gulch, but we fixed it."

"Good work. By the way, here's a letter for you, Roy. And I've some interesting mail, too." Mr. Manley winked genially at his sons.

"What's up, Dad?" Teddy inquired expectantly.

The ranch owner blew out a cloud of smoke and produced an envelope from the stack beside his plate.

"Best offer I've ever had for cattle, boys. From the biggest stockyard firm in the country, too." He grinned in satisfaction. "Who's your mail from, Roy?"

The older son seemed ready to burst with excitement. "Listen to this, everybody! It's from Ed Bartlett."

"Well, go ahead and spill it, Roy," urged his brother impatiently as the lad lapsed into a tense silence to scan the letter again.

"Must be very exciting, whatever it is," observed Mrs. Manley.

"It is!" Roy burst out. "Ed says his uncle is looking for a good ranch to use in his next moving picture and that he's thinking of ours!"

"Jumping coyotes!" Teddy exclaimed.

"I'll read what he says. 'Dear Roy, Uncle Hamilton——'"

"Hamilton Bartlett?" interrupted Mr. Manley inquiringly. "The famous producer? Is he really the uncle of your friend?"

"He certainly is, Dad! Listen: 'Uncle Hamilton needs a ranch for his next picture location, and from the description in your letter I thought that he might be interested in X Bar X. He said he had been dickering with the Z II outfit somewhere around your neighbourhood, but that he might look at your ranch before he makes up his mind. I'll let you know——'"

"What's that?" Teddy interrupted. "A plane!" he added, as a low throb, unmistakably an engine of some sort, sounded in the distance.

By the time the Manley family reached the front porch, nearly all hands on the ranch were gathered, gazing at an oncoming machine. The horses in the corral were growing restless. Pop Burns, the ranch foreman, came up, his grizzled face knotted into a scowl.

"Blasted buzzard!" he yelled, shaking his fist at the plane. "We'll be havin' a stampede any minute. These ponies ain't used to sech a racket."

The craft, arriving directly overhead, began to spiral downward slowly. The sound of the engine grew louder every second.

"Pretty tight spiral, if you ask me," Teddy observed. "Any tighter and the plane'll be in a spin!"

"I'll tell a maverick!" Roy agreed, watching the strange manœuvre with growing alarm. "It'll just about land where we're standing!"

The horses became wildly excited as the roar increased. Several of the cowboys ran for cover when it became evident that the plane now was in a tailspin, completely out of control.

Suddenly two tiny dots detached themselves from the falling craft. In a few seconds two parachutes mushroomed out in mid-air.

"They've jumped!" Roy cried as the ship, now pilotless, plummeted downward.

"Look out! Here she comes!" bellowed Pop Burns, diving for the open.

The other ranch hands, yelling and shouting, scattered in every direction. Mr. Manley seized his wife at the same instant that Roy grabbed Belle Ada. Everyone ran desperately from the danger zone.

For a sickening moment it looked as if the plane would land squarely in the corral, now seething with maddened horses. Then, just as the craft was about to hit, it gave a crazy lurch and hurtled into one end of the bunk-house.

There was a deafening crash and a burst of flame. This was followed by a scream of terror from within the demolished structure!

Chapter II

TO THE RESCUE

"It's Sing Lung! He's trapped!" Roy shouted.

Grabbing his brother by an arm, he made his way to the flaming bunk-house. The heat and smoke stopped them short.

"Help! Somebody come klick!" came a pitiful wail.

Nick ran up just then, carrying a pail of water. "We're starting a bucket brigade," he cried.

"Just what we need!" Roy exclaimed, seizing the container from the mystified cowboy. Ripping off his bandanna, the older Manley lad doused it in the water, his brother following his example. Both boys then tied the kerchiefs over their faces.

"You ain't a-goin' in *there*?" shouted Nick, his face frozen with horror. Before he could make a move to stop them, the two boys had plunged into the scorching smoke enveloping the bunk-house. No sooner had they disappeared than Mr. Manley ran up, his face white.

"Nick! Why didn't you——?"

"I—I couldn't stop 'em, Mr. Manley, but I ain't a-goin' to let you go in too!"

The boys' father made a desperate lunge toward the burning structure, but Nick Looker blocked his path.

"No sir-ee," he insisted.

The Manley boys repeatedly had shown courage and ability to handle situations requiring quick thinking and action. Bardwell Manley, their father and the owner

15

of the vast X Bar X ranch, had indeed trained his sons well.

The stalwart lads did not look alike. The older son, Roy, resembled his father, who was tall, heavy-set and dark. Teddy, a year younger than his brother, was inclined to be fair like his mother. Belle Ada, their only sister, was dark-eyed, fun-loving, and remarkably intelligent for her twelve years.

Many and varied are the experiences that have been encountered by the two boys. Their feats of horsemanship are common knowledge to everyone in that part of the West. They have saved lives and large amounts of money for persons who live in that section of the country. Their knowledge of cattle and the range has proved to be of the highest value in many times of stress. In the volume immediately preceding this one, entitled *The X Bar X Boys at Triangle Mine,* they rendered a valuable service to their father, though risking their lives to do so.

Returning to the scene in progress outside the blazing bunk-house, everything was confusion. The cowboys organised themselves into a bucket brigade. Nick, the man nearest the fire, tossed water on the flames as rapidly as pails could be handed down the line to him. The shouts of men and the screams of women made the din terrific.

"Come on! Speed up them pails!" Pop Burns cried out at the huddle of men around the well two hundred yards distant. The old rancher, his face set, was striding up and down along the line of cowboys. "That's right, Rad, shove that bucket along! Come on, Nat, get a move on. We've got to put that fire out and do it quick!"

Sweating in the terrific heat, and grimy with smoke

and cinders, the lads doubled their efforts. Mr. Manley, in the meantime, was struggling with Gus Tripp, who had taken Nick's place in an effort to prevent the desperate rancher from going into the fire after his sons.

"Please, Mr. Manley, you can't go in there!" the grizzled cowhand pleaded. "Things is bad enough now! The boys'll come out all right, one way or t'other."

Suddenly there was a yell from Nick. "The roof's collapsin'!"

"Never mind the roof! Keep a-throwin' them buckets like you never threw 'em before!" Pop Burns shouted encouragingly, though the veteran foreman knew as well as did his men that it was only a matter of minutes before the whole bunk-house would fall in.

Roy and his brother Teddy heard nothing of the hubbub outside. Hugging the floor of the kitchen, which they had managed to reach in a dash through the flames, they struggled toward the plaintive cries that sounded at intervals above the roar of the conflagration.

"He must be in the bunk-room!" Roy gasped as the two crawled through the dense smoke.

"We'll have to make it in a hurry!" shouted Teddy.

Just then the older Manley found himself at the door leading from the kitchen to the cowboys' sleeping-quarters. There he hesitated.

"Shall we open it, Ted?" he queried.

"Great Scott, we'll *have* to, draught or no draught! Go ahead."

A torrent of air rushed past them as Roy opened the door, the flames leaping wildly behind them.

"Look out, Ted!" his brother cried, glancing back. With a lightning grab he seized the lad and pulled him through the doorway just as the kitchen roof caved in with a splintering crash. Choking and gasping for breath, they peered around through the smoke in the bunk-room which as yet was not afire.

"Helpee! Sing Lung chokee!" came a cry from the far corner of the room. The boys dropped to the floor where the fumes were less dense, and crawled rapidly toward the Chinaman.

"You take one arm and I'll take the other, Ted," Roy managed to splutter. "We'll go out that door over there."

The cook lay huddled on the floor, holding a large frying-pan over his head. "Helpee!" was all he could say.

Half a minute later the brothers had dragged the frightened man to the open air, where he sank to the ground, still holding the cooking utensil over his head.

"It's all right, Sing Lung, you won't need the pan any more," said Roy, who had to laugh, despite the seriousness of the situation. "Let's take a look at you. Are you hurt?"

"Me chokee blurn to dleath. Velly hot!"

"I think you're not much hotter than we are," Teddy remarked. "Can you move all right?"

It required some persuasion before Sing Lung would believe that he actually was alive and safe and no longer needed the frying-pan as a helmet. Suddenly the brothers realised from the shouting that they were being sought. Quickly they ran to the other side of the bunk-house, where they were greeted by a lusty cry.

"They're safe, men, and they got Sing Lung out, too!"

A whoop of joy rang through the bucket brigade, for

the cowboys to a man were fond of the Manley brothers. Their father drew a relieved breath.

"Thank goodness!" he said. "You'd better go up to the house now."

"Nothing doing, Dad. We're all right. What about those fellows in the plane? Has anybody found them?" Teddy queried.

"Been too busy tryin' to put out the fire," Nick chimed in. "I think we've got 'er under control now, but it looks like we'll need a new bunk-house kitchen."

Although the air was still dense with smoke, the flames had subsided, leaving one end of the structure a charred mass of debris. From it the metal propeller of the burned aeroplane protruded crazily.

"Funny thing those parachute jumpers haven't turned up yet," Teddy speculated.

"Let's ride out and look for them," Roy suggested. "They may have been hurt."

In a jiffy the boys had saddled their ponies and headed for the sage-dotted plain.

"The question is where to look," said Roy. "Say, what's the matter with that herd of cattle over there?"

He pointed toward a cluster of steers about a quarter of a mile distant.

"They seem to be restless or something," Teddy replied. "Well, here goes!"

Nudging their horses with their knees, the brothers took off at a gallop and soon reached the herd. Obviously something was wrong, for the stock were pawing the ground restlessly and churning about.

"Well, I still don't see——" Roy began.

Teddy broke in with a shout. "Look, Roy, isn't that a parachute?"

A large white object lay spread out on the ground several yards away, partly tangled in sagebrush. In a twinkling the brothers dismounted and hurried to investigate.

"Roy, look!"

The hearts of the brothers skipped beats as Teddy pointed to a twisted mass of rope leading from the huge parachute directly into the herd of milling cattle near by. The evidence left no doubt.

"Do you suppose the person has been trampled?" Roy asked with a queer feeling in the pit of his stomach.

"We'll soon find out. I think if we ride into the herd carefully enough——"

Quickly the older Manley lad climbed into his saddle. "When I give the signal, Ted, you pull on those ropes as fast as you can."

"Right. Here's hoping."

Gently Roy urged his pony, Star, into the herd of steers, which were growing more unruly each minute. The lad, wise in the ways of cattle, knew that the slightest unnatural movement at this point would result instantly in a stampede from which the boys would be lucky to come out alive.

"See anything yet?" Teddy called anxiously.

"No. Golly, this rope I'm following must be a mile long!"

Roy urged Star in farther. Suddenly, almost beneath his pony's hoofs, he caught sight of a man's figure huddled on the ground.

Chapter III

A DANGEROUS CLIMB

"Did you find him?" cried Teddy.

"Yes. But I don't know how I'm going to get him out."

Roy gazed around anxiously at the cattle, expecting a steer's hoof to land on the motionless figure at any moment. Furthermore, it was impossible for Roy to dismount without running the same risk himself.

"Shall I start pulling the rope?" called his brother.

"Not yet. Wait until I see if I can clear a path."

Gingerly, Roy steered his horse around the man and surveyed the situation again.

"No use trying our original plan, Ted," he called at length. "Only one thing to do, and that's to get this fellow on Star."

"Wait a second, Roy. I'll ride Flash in and see if we can clear a little more space."

The situation was perilous. To make any sort of hurried move would be folly, as the steers already were showing signs of an impending stampede.

A moment later Teddy followed his brother into the herd. Reaching Roy, he wheeled his mount Flash about twice, jostling the cattle as far as possible from the motionless aviator on the ground.

"All right, Ted, watch that ugly-looking fellow over there," said Roy, indicating a huge animal a few feet from them.

Holding Star steady, the older Manley lad slipped

from the saddle. At the same instant he leaped aside as
the giant steer pawed menacingly. Teddy in the meantime manœuvred Flash about the tiny space in a skilful
attempt to give his brother room.

With a heave Roy picked up the unconscious flyer
and placed him across the saddle. A second later he was
on Star's back, holding the motionless body with one
hand and the reins with the other.

"Good work!" Teddy said tensely. "All set?"

"Right."

With his brother in the lead, Roy cautiously guided
Star through the herd, holding the victim on his pre-
carious perch with all the strength in his aching fist.
Two minutes later they were safe.

"Boy, that was a close call!" Teddy exploded with
relief. "Is the man hurt?"

Roy dismounted and laid the flyer on the ground.
"A few scratches, but I can't find anything else wrong.
His pulse is beating all right."

"Just a faint, perhaps. Can't say that I blame him,
either. Maybe if we loosen up some of his clothes he'll
—say, did you hear that?"

A weird, choking cry sounded near by, followed a
second later by another.

"Seems to be coming from that cottonwood," Roy
decided, pointing to a single large tree several hundred
yards away.

"I'll go have a look," offered his brother.

The younger lad galloped away while Roy began
attempts to revive the unconscious flyer. The dull
thump of hoofs announced a newcomer. Nick Looker
thundered up to a stop.

"Well, I'll be hit by a prairie dog if it ain't you playin'

nursemaid ag'in!" drawled the cowboy. "Who is he? One o' them parachute fellers?"

"Good guess, Nick. How about taking him back to the ranch? He needs help right away."

"Roy!" came a shout, as Teddy galloped back. "Follow me! Quick!"

Without waiting for an answer, the boy turned Flash about and was off again in the direction of the cottonwood tree.

"Take care of this fellow, Nick!" Roy cried, leaping on Star and following his brother until they reached the cottonwood tree.

"It's the other flyer, Roy. He's caught by the windpipe."

Simultaneously the boys sprang to the ground and shinned up the gnarled trunk. High above them in the branches dangled the second flyer, emitting queer choking sounds.

"I climbed up before, but I couldn't get him loose," Teddy explained rapidly. "Come with me."

Quickly the two brothers ascended. Near the top of the tree they found an elderly man, dressed in smart business clothes, wedged tightly among the branches in such a manner that his windpipe was almost shut off. His breathing had practically ceased.

"We'll have to work fast, Ted. Here, grab that branch and pull it for all you're worth."

"Wait. Suppose he drops through?"

"I'm going to hold him. Ready?"

Roy slipped to a lower branch and obtained a secure hold on the victim's legs.

"All right, Ted."

The man's neck was caught in a fork of limbs. It was

one of these that Teddy was endeavouring to break off. Summoning every ounce of his strength, he pulled. Suddenly the branch gave way. With a sickening crash the younger Manley lad lost his hold and plummeted downward.

Roy had scant time to realise Teddy's predicament, for the flyer's head had been released and the body had fallen on him. The older Manley boy now found himself balancing precariously in a network of branches, a man's full weight upon him.

"Ted! Are you all right?" he shouted finally.

Fortunately his brother had managed to stop his fall before he hit the ground. Now, save for a few scratches and a dazed feeling, he was none the worse for the experience.

"I'm O.K., Roy. Hold on, I'll be right up."

It was slow and tedious work lowering the unconscious form still enmeshed in the cords of the huge parachute which ballooned out over the top of the tree. Carefully the lads severed the ropes and eased the man down from branch to branch. Nearly a half-hour elapsed before they reached the ground.

"I can't feel any pulse at all, Ted," said his brother.

"You stay here with him, Roy, and I'll—hello, here comes somebody. Nick!"

The familiar figure of the young cowboy had appeared suddenly astride his bay mare.

"Got the other one, eh?" He dismounted and came over. "He looks pretty well gone to me. Rad's comin' with the buckboard in a minute. I sort of figgered it'd be easier ridin' after the time I had gettin' that other fellow to the ranch."

"How is he, anyhow?" Roy queried.

"Oh, he's comin' round. Pretty scared, but your dad went over him and couldn't find anything busted."

There was nothing to do at the moment but to wait for Rad Sell, one of the ranch hands.

"Who do you suppose these fellows are?" Roy speculated.

"Probably rustlers," Nick suggested. "Ain't nobody else in these parts flyin' around in those two-man jobs."

"Nick, you should have been a lawyer," Teddy said ironically. "You'd make a fortune hanging people without even putting them on the stand!"

The handsome cowboy smiled. "Mebbe so, Ted, but I think we'd not be takin' much of a chance with these fellers. They're rustlers, sure as you're livin' on a ranch. Didn't ya notice the other one? Young fellow, 'bout thirty. Dressed like a city slicker, same as this'n is. That's the way the rustlers look nowadays, like honest business men."

Roy grunted. "Well, rustler or no rustler, here comes the ambulance."

There was a clatter in the distance as a large wagon appeared, bouncing wildly behind a galloping horse. Weaving in and out among the cottonwood trees and sagebrush, it rapidly approached.

"W-h-o-a, there!" sang out a lusty voice as Rad Sell drew up beside them. "Hello, what's up?" He jumped down from his perch on the buckboard. "The other buzzard, eh?"

"Give us a hand, Rad, he's in a bad way," said Nick. Despite his remarks of a few minutes ago, he lost no time now that the wagon had arrived. Gently they lifted up the unfortunate flyer and placed him on a pile of saddle blankets in the back of the vehicle. Roy and

Teddy climbed in with him while Rad returned to the driver's seat.

"See you later," called Nick. "I'll bring in the horses."

The condition of their patient made it necessary for them to proceed slowly. It was nearly fifteen minutes later when they drew up to the door of Bardwell Manley's home. The owner was awaiting them, a stranger beside him.

"This is Mr. Morris Fort, the pilot," their father said. "Judging from the looks of your patient here, we'd better do something in a hurry."

Nick, eyeing the airman suspiciously, helped the boys carry the second flyer into the house, where Mr. Manley promptly administered first aid. In a few moments the elderly man began to show signs of life. Presently his eyelids flickered open.

"Wh-why, where am I? Fort! What's the matter? Are we falling? Fort! *Do* something before we crash!" He gazed around him dazedly.

"There, now, you're all right," soothed Mr. Manley. "Just lie still."

The victim made an effort to pull himself together.

"We've crashed already, Mr. Bartlett, but things are all right now," the pilot cut in.

Roy started in surprise. "Mr. Bartlett, did you say?"

"He's Hamilton Bartlett, the movie producer," Fort whispered. "We were on our way to pay you a visit when it happened."

Teddy flushed with excitement and Nick Looker promptly lost his cynical expression. Mr. Bartlett was gazing around expectantly.

"I feel a little better now," he said in a weak voice.

"What's that you say, Fort? Did we really crash? Was anybody—were you hurt?"

"No, I'm all right, thanks to these two young fellows." The pilot indicated Roy and Teddy. "They rescued me from a herd of cattle and pulled you out of a tree, so I hear."

"I'm Bardwell Manley. These are my sons, Roy and Teddy," the ranchman explained. "Now I think you'd better try to sleep for a while."

"Manley? Bardwell Manley? Are you the owner of— what was the name of it—oh, yes, the X Bar X ranch?" the producer exclaimed. "Now I remember everything! We were just about to land. I came here to make you a proposition. You see, my company needs a ranch-setting for their next picture." He paused for breath while the boys waited excitedly.

"My young nephew has told me all about your sons and your ranch, and if what he said is correct, I think your outfit will just about suit our purpose; that is, if you're willing."

"Willing!" Teddy burst out. "Jumping coyotes, it would be wonderful!"

Chapter IV

ONE-ARM KOSTY

Supper that evening was a noisy affair, with everybody at the table talking at once. Mr. Manley had given his consent for the motion picture to be filmed at X Bar X.

"What do you suppose the name of it is going to be?" Roy wondered.

"It'll be 'The X Bar X Mystery', of course," Teddy assured him. "And probably Sing Lung will be the villain."

"Not if *he* knows it," laughed his brother. "I was talking to him about it a few minutes before supper and he's all upset. Afraid they're going to make an actor of him."

"What I'd like to know is what caused the wreck," Bardwell Manley interposed. "Or would you rather not talk about it, Mr. Fort?"

The pilot frowned reflectively, then looked up. "I don't mind talking about it, Mr. Manley. The point is, I'm wondering myself just what happened. I didn't say anything about it before, but prior to the crash we landed at another ranch. Mr. Bartlett, I believe, wanted to look it over for picture possibilities."

"What place was that, Mr. Fort?" Roy asked.

"I was just trying to remember. I think it was called the X II, or Z something or other."

"Z II," corrected Roy. "It's several miles south of here."

"Yes, that must have been the one. Anyhow, we landed near the ranch and went inside to inquire about the place. Two cowboys were sitting there, a fat one and a fellow with only one arm."

"One-Arm Kosty," Teddy exclaimed. "He's—pardon me for interrupting, Mr. Fort."

"Quite all right. Do you know him?"

"Everybody around here knows him. He's the caretaker on the ranch. Hasn't the best reputation in the world."

"Well, as I was saying," the pilot continued, "we introduced ourselves and told them we were thinking of using their ranch in a movie Mr. Bartlett was planning to make. After we'd looked around and talked to them some more, I could see Mr. Bartlett didn't care much for them."

"And then?" Roy was tense with excitement.

"Well, he finally told them he wouldn't use their ranch. The one-armed fellow muttered something about not getting his wages raised, and walked out. Later we saw him standing beside our plane, but as soon as we showed ourselves he ran off."

"Sounds mighty suspicious to me," said Teddy.

"I'll tell a maverick," Roy exclaimed. "Things always look suspicious when Kosty's around."

The pilot frowned. "I didn't think much about it until, well, until after the crash. As we flew over your ranch and I was looking for a landing place something went wrong with the controls. The ship wouldn't respond, a condition that just doesn't happen to a new plane. First thing we knew we were in a spin and there wasn't a thing to do about it."

Teddy scratched his head. "If I'm not mistaken, wasn't it the Z II outfit, Roy, that——"

"Gee, I'd forgotten!" his brother exclaimed. "That's the ranch Ed Bartlett mentioned in his letter. Said his uncle had considered it for the picture. Isn't that right, Mr. Fort?"

The aviator shook his head. "I really couldn't say. You see, I'm just Mr. Bartlett's personal pilot."

He was interrupted by the sudden appearance of Hamilton Bartlett.

"Mind if I join you?" He smiled pleasantly at the group around the table.

"Whew, you certainly recover quickly!" Mr. Manley exclaimed, rising and pulling up an extra chair. "Here, make yourself comfortable. Norine!"

The pretty young girl came from the kitchen.

"Please bring a plate for Mr. Bartlett," said Mrs. Manley. She turned to the producer. "We were just hearing about your crash."

"Well, I'm no detective, but I have a few ideas about all this." The film executive's grey eyes snapped. It was evident that the man, elderly though he was, could not be trifled with. "I suppose Fort has told you about our landing at Z II and the one-armed fellow."

"Yes, I told them, Mr. Bartlett," the pilot nodded. "From what the boys say I think we'd have been better off if we'd chosen some other ranch on which to land."

The clatter of hoof-beats sounded outside. A moment later two girls, nattily dressed in riding clothes, burst into the Manley dining-room.

"Well, of all things. Hello, Curley!" exclaimed Teddy, jumping up. "Hello, Nell!"

For a moment excitement ran high as the family greeted Ethel Carew, or Curley, as she liked to be called, and Nell Willis, her cousin. These two girls had just come from New York on one of their frequent visits to their aunt, Mrs. Peter Ball, whose husband owned the 8 X 8 ranch not far from X Bar X.

"We heard about the aeroplane crash and the fire!" Nell chattered excitedly, "and we could hardly wait to ride over."

"Was anybody hurt?" her cousin inquired anxiously. "One of the cowboys said two men had to jump out with parachutes!"

Mrs. Manley hastened to introduce the producer and his pilot. At mention of Hamilton Bartlett's name and his proposition the girls were thrilled.

"Everybody for miles around will be flocking here to see a real movie being made!" Nell squealed. "What's the picture to be called, Mr. Bartlett, or is the title a secret?"

"It's the 'X Bar X Mystery', of course!" Teddy chimed in, whereupon the producer smiled.

"Well, you almost guessed right, Ted. We're going to call the picture 'The Sagebrush Mystery', and from all the assistance we're to have," and Mr. Bartlett gazed around with a twinkle in his eye, "I think it will be the best production we've ever made!"

When supper was over, Roy and Teddy immediately rushed the girls out to see the bunk-house before darkness should come on. Mr. Manley and Hamilton Bartlett lingered to talk over the details of the forthcoming picture.

"We'll pay you damages in addition to your price for allowing us to use your ranch as a setting," the producer said, "and I want to do something for your boys. After all, they saved two lives this afternoon."

Mr. Manley laughed. "They were glad to do it, I'm sure, and they'll not be looking for rewards."

"Certainly not, Mr. Manley, but we'll see. In the meantime I'd like to ask a favour, though we've imposed on you enough as it is!"

The hearty ranch owner waved his hand. "Forget it, Bartlett. What can I do for you?"

"I'd like to use the bunk-house just as it is, at least for the first part of the picture. Can you get along for a few weeks without repairing the burned portion? I'll explain our whole idea."

As the two men drew up their chairs before the fireside to continue their discussion, Roy and Teddy stood out by the bunk-house with the girls, watching an approaching horseman.

"Looks familiar," Teddy remarked. "By golly, he's One-Arm Kosty! What do you suppose he wants?"

"Who is One-Arm Kosty?" Nell queried curiously.

"Caretaker over at Mrs. Slater's ranch, the Z II," Roy said tensely. A moment later a coal-black mare galloped up to them, foaming heavily. The rider, a thin, hard-looking fellow with a crooked smile, swung himself off with his single arm.

"Evenin', folks." The voice, like its owner, was rasping and offensive.

"Hello, Kosty," Roy said coolly. "What can we do for you?"

"Heared ye had a little trouble this arternoon." The cowboy's lips curled and snaked into an ugly sneer.

"Oh, nothin' in p'ticular," he drawled. He eyed them narrowly for an instant, then continued, "Hear ye're goin' to be big movie folks."

Knowing One-Arm Kosty's reputation in the county, Roy and his brother sensed the fellow had some ulterior motive for his visit.

"Yore old man around?" he asked.

Before the boys could reply there came the sound of voices approaching them.

"I think your proposition is satisfactory," Mr. Manley was saying. "You understand, of course, that our regular work here must not be interrupted. Hello! Visitor, eh?"

In the rapidly growing darkness Mr. Manley and the producer, talking earnestly, had not noticed the fellow before.

"This is Mr. Kosty, Dad," Roy cut in. "He says he wants to see you."

"That so? Show him inside, Roy. Mr. Bartlett and I want to look over some of our buildings before it gets too dark."

Reluctantly, the older Manley lad escorted the hard-faced fellow into his father's study, where they sat in silence. At length footfalls sounded on the front porch and a moment later the ranch owner and Bartlett came in.

"Do you want to see me alone?" Mr. Manley inquired gruffly of their visitor.

"If it's all the same to you, I'd like to have Mr. Bartlett come in too," Kosty smiled. "Howdy-do, Mr. Bartlett? Remember me?"

The producer scowled. "I believe so, I believe so,"

he said impatiently. "You say you want to see me now?"

Kosty uncrossed his legs and stood up lazily. "It's like this, men. You was a-goin' to use the Z II ranch for that there picture of yours. Is that right?"

Bartlett nodded. "We had considered using the Z II," he replied, "but I don't remember having discussed the idea with you. Are you the owner of Z II?" He eyed Kosty sharply, but the other showed no sign of being ill-at-ease.

"No, I ain't exactly the owner, but I do most of the advisin'. The point is, Mr. Bartlett, that we got equipment you need. Understand you want a corral 'bout twice't the size of the one here."

"I think the X Bar X corral will do very nicely," said the producer coldly.

Kosty smiled in his irritating manner. "Understand you need a hundred horses and cowboys to ride 'em. Ain't half that many on X Bar X."

Bartlett cleared his throat in embarrassment. "Manley, why don't you escort this person to the door?"

The ranch owner grunted. "Let him have his say, Bartlett. Maybe he's right. Perhaps you'll do better at the Z II, for they're a bigger outfit, no doubt about it."

Kosty smiled triumphantly. "Understand you want to show a rodeo, Mr. Bartlett, ain't that right? Well, we're a-plannin' the biggest one ever held in these parts three weeks from now. Just about suit ye, wouldn't it?"

Roy was fairly bursting with indignation. "Funny thing nobody's heard of it before," he observed.

Disregarding Roy's remark, Kosty reached for his sombrero. "Wal, jes' thought I'd drop in and tell ye a few things as might help your pi'ture, Mr. Bartlett. Any time ye'd like to drop over and look at what we got——" He hesitated at the doorway, his beady eyes glittering. A moment later he was gone.

Mr. Manley broke the tense silence that followed Kosty's departure. "It's up to you, Bartlett. Don't feel obligated——"

The producer shrugged. "It isn't that, Manley. Of course, business is business. I've got to find the ranch that will fit into the picture best, whether I like it or not."

The study door suddenly swung open and Teddy came in, breathless.

"Dad! Nick just came back from Crooked Gulch. There's a break in the fence down there. Steers running through like buckshot!"

Roy and his father jumped to their feet simultaneously. "Get Pop Burns right away, Ted!" Mr. Manley rapped out.

"Crooked Gulch! We went over every inch of that wire yesterday!" Roy exclaimed.

Nick flung open the door, closely followed by Pop Burns. Both were highly excited.

"It's a put-up job, Mr. Manley, shore as shootin'!" Nick fumed.

"Never mind, get out the men!" thundered the ranch owner. "If this is a rustling job somebody's going to pay for it!"

"The men are leavin' now," Pop Burns cut in. "I ordered a round-up soon's Nick come in."

Without waiting to hear more, Roy and Teddy dashed out to the corral.

"I'll bet a good lasso this is One-Arm Kosty's work," the younger Manley panted as he and his brother raced down the path. "Nick says the wire was *cut*!"

Chapter V.

A STICK OF DYNAMITE

"Kiyi! Kiyi!"

The air was filled with the shouts of cowboys and the thunder of flying hoofs. Teddy and Roy, jumping on their ponies, were off with the others in a twinkling.

"Nick says the wire was cut!" Roy exclaimed as they galloped along side by side.

"Yes. And if One-Arm Kosty didn't do it I'll eat a prairie dog for breakfast."

"Don't think you'll have to, for probably you're right. Wait till you hear what happened in Dad's study just before you came in."

Teddy scowled as his brother related the incident. "If that groundhog is out to make trouble for us he'd better watch his step!"

There was a yell from behind, as a flashlight beam cut through the darkness. A galloping horseman overtook them.

"Wal, ef it ain't you two!"

"Hello, Ranny!" called Roy. "Coming to the picnic?"

"Right!" responded the good-looking young cowboy. "So's your Pop. He was jest gettin' on General when I come through the gate."

Directly in front of them, about half a mile away, a cluster of moving lights could be seen. Dim shadows of horsemen crossed to and fro in the rays.

"See you later!" Ranny shouted, suddenly veering off as they approached the weird scene of a round-up by flashlight. In a second he was swallowed in the confusion of horses and steers dashing about madly. Roy and Teddy quickly followed him into the thick of things.

"Fence must be down for half a mile!" the older Manley boy yelled at his brother. "We'd better ride through and head off the cattle."

Pop Burns suddenly rode up, pointing his light in their faces.

"Roy, go after the strays! Ted, follow me, quick!"

As the two galloped toward the leaders of the stampede, Roy wheeled Star off into the blackness to search for steers that had become separated from the main herd. There were plenty of them. Each time he would catch sight of one in his flashlight beam he would thunder down on the frightened beast and head it back toward the broken fence.

Teddy and Pop meanwhile had joined the main group of cowboys far out on the prairie where hard riding and yelling finally had broken the stampede. Gradually the steers were turned about and driven toward the X Bar X side of the fence.

"Man down!" suddenly rang out through the night.

Instinctively Teddy let out a cry as a horse stumbled and fell in front of him. Its rider, hurtling through the air, landed a scant few feet from the nearest steer. Instantly young Manley vaulted from his saddle and dragged the figure to safety not a second too soon.

"Ranny!"

Dazedly, the cowboy blinked in Teddy's light, then gingerly felt of his shoulder.

"Ouch!" he muttered. "Must o' broke somethin'."

"What's happened?" crackled a hoarse voice from

the darkness. It was that of Pop Burns, always turning up at crucial moments.

"It's his shoulder, Pop," Teddy responded. "I'll tie it up so it'll hold till he gets back."

"Can you make it, Ranny?" the veteran puncher asked solicitously. "Ted, you'd better ride along with 'im. We won't need you around here no longer, for the fun's about over, I'm glad to say." Jumping back on his dappled mare, he galloped off.

Ranny, his shoulder trussed up in Ted's bandanna, managed to mount his horse. With the Manley lad riding beside him he headed homeward.

"Heard any rumours about the fence bein' cut, Teddy?"

"I've an idea who did it, Ranny. One-Arm Kosty."

The injured man frowned blackly. "You really think so? Maybe it was that skunk! Never did have much use fer 'im, even if old Mrs. Slater does think he's the trustiest waddy on her ranch."

"He was around after supper trying to talk Mr. Bartlett into making his movie over there on Z II," Teddy remarked. "Of course, that doesn't make him guilty, but he's pretty sore about X Bar X getting the contract. Another thing: he rode up from Crooked Gulch direction where the fence was cut."

Ranny clucked his tongue. "Oh, he did, did he? What was he doin' down by Crooked Gulch? That's the longest way around from his place to ours!"

"Of course. Looks suspicious to me. Roy feels the same way."

"Well, all I got to say is, if One-Arm Kosty cut that fence he'll have a powerful lot o' reckonin' to do with me!"

Half an hour later the lighted windows of the ranch-house came into view. Soon the young men reached the corral, where Teddy turned in their horses.

"Come into the bunk-house, or what's left of it, and I'll fix your shoulder," the Manley lad suggested. In an improvised 'operatin'-room', as Ranny laughingly called it, Teddy manipulated the injured shoulder into place as he had often seen his father do, and strapped it securely.

"There now, you'll be riding as well as ever in a week," he declared, surveying the bandage.

"Thanks, Doctor," Ranny smiled. "See you later."

The Manley lad reached the ranch-house just as his father, accompanied by Mr. Bartlett, clumped up the front steps and stamped the dust from his boots.

"Hello, Teddy. How's Ranny? Heard he was hurt."

"He's all right, Dad. Had a dislocated shoulder, which I strapped. Mr. Bartlett, don't tell me *you* were in the round-up!"

The elderly producer, attired in chaps and sombrero, was smiling proudly.

"Sure!" he exclaimed. "Why not? Besides, I think I've discovered a couple of new movie stars."

Teddy looked at the white-haired executive inquiringly, as the man's smile grew broader.

"If the pictures I took of you and your brother riding a little while ago turn out as well as I think they will——"

"Pictures? Of Roy and me?"

Just then the older Manley came up from the corral. "Hello—what's all the conference?" he inquired.

His father laughed through the stubby stem of his corn-cob pipe. "I'll have to admit it myself—you two whippersnappers did some mighty fine riding to-night. It's a good thing you did, too, for our friend Mr. Bartlett was taking moving pictures of you a big part of the time!"

"Maybe I'd better explain matters a bit, Manley," laughed the producer. "I think your sons don't believe what we're telling them. Boys, I happened to take a flashlight movie camera down to the round-up and saw enough of both of you to crank off some shots that ought to be good. We'll find out in the morning."

The excitement of the round-up, coupled with suspense over the films, made sleep difficult for Roy and Teddy that night. The crack of dawn found them up and dressed. To their surprise Mr. Bartlett greeted them in the dining-room, where he was studying a strip of photographic film.

"It's wonderful, boys! Wonderful, I say! Come here and have a look!"

Before they could recover from their surprise, the Manleys found themselves viewing a record of their part in the round-up.

"Of course, you can't see much looking at a film," the producer apologised, "so I've made a few prints of the best shots. Here!"

To the boys he handed a small stack of positive plates which they had not noticed lying on the table.

"Golly!" Roy gulped. "You're—you're not going to use these in the movie——?"

"I certainly am!" said Bartlett emphatically. "They're among the best pictures of action riding I've ever seen. Look at those horses! Look at you two there! That's *action*! It's just what I want for 'The Sagebrush Mystery'. How about it?"

"How about it? How about what?" Teddy wondered.

"How about you two taking real parts in the picture? Title roles, I mean. I'll give you copies of the script. You can learn your parts in no time at all. We'll discuss terms when your father comes down."

"Golly, Mr. Bartlett, we'll never be able to thank you——" Roy began, but the producer waved him aside.

"My goodness, fellows, *you're* the ones to be thanked! Didn't you save my life and Fort's? Anything I can do for you after that will be less than you deserve."

The brothers could hardly wait until the rest of the family came down to breakfast.

"Well, Bartlett," beamed Mr. Manley after hearing the news, "if you really think my sons will do, it's all right with me."

"Gee, you're lucky!" Belle Ada exclaimed, wide-eyed, whereupon the producer laughed and patted the girl's curls.

"Maybe we'll find a place for you too, little lady," he said. "In the meantime," he added, turning to Mr. Manley, "my equipment should be here now. I had it sent on before we left."

"It's probably at the freight station in Eagles, the nearest town," Roy chimed in.

"Suppose my brother and I ride over and see about it," said Teddy excitedly. "How about it, Roy?"

Ten minutes after breakfast Nick and the Manleys were perched on the high seat of the ranch wagon, heading toward the little village of Eagles, twelve miles distant.

"So ye're a-goin' to be big movie stars now, eh?"

drawled Nick as the three bounced along the rough road. "Wal, more power to ye!"

Teddy pursed his lips thoughtfully. "I've a hunch things aren't going to be as easy as they sound. If One-Arm Kosty isn't out to make trouble for us, I miss my guess."

"And you ain't usually wrong," Nick observed significantly.

They rode the rest of the way in silence, each vowing to find out whether or not the sinister-looking caretaker had been responsible for cutting the fence and turning loose thousands of X Bar X cattle.

"Eagles ahead!" Roy sang out an hour later. "Hope Andy's awake and knows if Mr. Bartlett's equipment has come in."

Presently they wheeled around a corner and drew up alongside an old shed by the railroad tracks. A stocky individual in dusty chaps sat nodding in the sun.

"Bug-Eye, of all people!" Roy yelped, jumping out. "Hey, there, wake up!"

The slumbering cowpuncher sat up suddenly and opened his eyes. "Wal, look who's here!" he croaked. "Jes' the waddies I was a-waitin' fer. Hear X Bar X is a-goin' in the movies."

"Bet your life, Bug-Eye," Teddy laughed. "Better come over and see the fun."

"Before I do that, boys, I'm aimin' to have you 'uns over to 8 X 8 to see the new camera I invented. Soon's I heared about somebody makin' movies at your outfit I said to m'self, 'Bug-Eye, thar's yore big chance!' So I ups and invents a camera. Wait'll you see 'er!"

"Another invention, really?" Roy laughed.

The boys had enjoyed many a joke at the expense of

their good-natured if somewhat eccentric friend, whose hobby consisted of inventing strange devices for many purposes.

"Yep," said Bug-Eye, "another invention. And she's the best one yet!"

Promising to visit the 8 X 8 ranch and see the new camera as soon as they could, the Manleys set about finding Andy, the station master. The man promptly led them to a stack of crates and boxes.

"Here y'are, boys. Better be keerful, though, fer some o' them boxes is marked 'dynamite'."

Half an hour later the wagon was loaded and the three from X Bar X set out for home.

"Wonder what all the dynamite's fer," Nick grunted, gingerly holding the reins. "Can't say as I like the idea o' bangin' over rough trails and bein' blowed to pieces fer the trouble."

Despite the cowboy's misgivings, he and the Manleys reached the ranch without any inconvenience, to find Mr. Bartlett watching for them.

"Good!" exclaimed the producer, peering into the wagon. "Well, let's not waste any time. Nick, will you have some of the men help you unload—and then come back here? I want to see you."

Mystified, the young man summoned several of the ranch hands who soon had the crates neatly stacked in a corner of the bunk-house.

"Fine!" commended Bartlett, following them around eagerly. The producer, now that work was ready to begin, was a bundle of nervous energy. "Nick, I want you to open that box marked 'Number 6' and put on the Indian costume you'll find inside. Roy, you and Teddy help me set up the camera."

Nick, who was too astonished to ask questions, did as he was told and emerged timidly from the bunkhouse a few minutes later in full Indian regalia. The Manleys, in the meantime, had unpacked the complicated movie camera and placed it according to Bartlett's directions near the corral.

"Say, you're a better-looking chief than I thought you'd be!" the producer exclaimed as Nick approached them amid a chorus of cat-calls from the crowd of cowboys who had gathered to watch the proceedings.

"Wal, I can't say as I feel like one," Nick smiled foolishly. "What am I s'posed to do now, Mr. Bartlett?"

"Just walk up and down in front of the camera," the producer ordered. "I want to get a few shots of you for the first part of the picture. Look fierce!"

The cowboy peered around uncomfortably.

"You don't look fierce enough!" shouted Bartlett. "Make a face! Look tough! All right, Roy, turn the crank. Keep the lens trained on him."

For ten minutes Nick paraded up and down before the camera while Roy, under the producer's watchful eye, cranked the apparatus.

"All right, that's enough," said Bartlett. "You can take off the duds, Nick. Come on, boys, I want to shoot some prairie scenes. We'll load the camera on the wagon."

The brothers were fascinated with the duties of filming a movie, especially under the direction of such an energetic man. Quickly stowing the equipment in the ranch wagon, they climbed up on the seat with Bartlett between them.

"Don't know what's happened to all my gang. Guess they got lost on the way," the producer remarked as they started out. "That won't stop us from making a few easy shots in the meantime."

Half a mile along the trail toward Crooked Gulch, Roy suddenly pointed across the sage-dotted prairie.

"Look!" he cried.

A horseman in Indian dress was racing off into the distance at full gallop.

"I've a hunch that's not Nick!" Teddy muttered tensely. "Because—here comes Nick now!"

Chapter VI

A STRANGE COINCIDENCE

"Mr. Bartlett! Somebody stole my Injun suit!" Nick Looker cried breathlessly, reining up beside the three in the ranch wagon.

"And there he goes off th—— Why, he's disappeared!" Roy interrupted himself, staring in consternation at the spot on the sage-dotted prairie where the strange horseman had been an instant before.

Nick looked around in great bewilderment. "Where? Who's disappeared?"

"The fellow who stole your Indian suit," Roy explained hastily. "We just saw him riding hard in that direction."

"He can't be far off!" Teddy cut in. "Nick, you better go after him. Come on, Roy, let's get Star and Flash and help hunt."

Leaving the puzzled cowboy to canter off in the direction Teddy had indicated, the brothers wheeled the wagon about and raced back to the ranch.

"I don't care so much about the suit, but there was a stick of dynamite in one of the side pockets," Bartlett shouted over the clatter. "Somebody's likely to be blown up if he's not careful!"

When they reached the corral both boys leaped to the ground simultaneously.

"See you later," Roy called to the producer as they mounted their ponies.

In a few seconds the brothers were thundering across the plain toward a tiny figure on horseback half a mile or so distant.

"Poor Nick, he's probably wondering what everything's about," Roy laughed. "We didn't have much time to explain matters."

Teddy snorted. "We'll probably have plenty of time now. It's like looking for a needle in a haystack, trying to find that fellow at this point."

"He'll probably head for Rocky Gulch."

The rider ahead waved and galloped up to meet them.

"See anything, Nick?" Roy panted.

The cowboy shook his head. "Nope. I just climbed that cottonwood tree, too, fer a good look-around. Ef thar's an Injun around here I cain't see 'im."

"What happened, Nick?" Teddy inquired. "Did anybody see the fellow steal the suit?"

"Wal, it was thisaway. I took the duds off in the bunk-house and then I went out to the pump fer a drink. First thing I know I see somebody with my Injun suit on ridin' past me so fast he was blurred. I yelled to the boys, but they was busy lookin' at Mr. Bartlett's equipment and didn't pay no attention. By the time I got on Sally, here, the fellow'd disappeared in the brush, so I rode out to your wagon."

"Nick, you take the trail toward Smoky Creek while Ted and I head for Rocky Gulch," Roy suggested. "The thief must be one place or the other."

"Right by me, boys. I'll fire three shots if I ketch the bird."

Nick, spurring his horse, was off in a dusty swirl. The brothers picked up the rough trail leading toward

Rocky Gulch. Suddenly, at the top of a knoll, Roy held up his hand.

"Look, Teddy. There's the fellow!"

A quarter of a mile ahead of them, in a shallow valley, a horseman in Indian dress was approaching.

Teddy frowned. "Something queer about it, Roy. Why is he coming this way?"

They watched in puzzled silence as the figure came closer.

"Some sort of a trick, Ted, sure as you're born."

Just then the stranger turned abruptly from the trail to be swallowed up in the growth along the side.

"I thought so!" Roy interjected. "Come on. After him!"

They raced down the rocky path to a point where the strange figure had disappeared. Not ten yards from the edge of the trail was the fugitive, placidly watering his horse in a small brook. He regarded the brothers calmly.

"Who are you?" Teddy demanded, jumping to the ground and walking toward him, with Roy at his heels.

"Me White Feather."

The man was a magnificent specimen of a real Indian. Tall, aristocratic, calm, bedecked in head-dress and trinkets of all colours, he was a typical chieftain. The brothers, however, were still suspicious.

"We'd better search him, Teddy."

"Right. Put up your hands, White Feather, or whatever your name is," the younger lad ordered impulsively.

The Indian obeyed without the flicker of an eyelash, while Roy's quick inspection revealed nothing that resembled a stick of dynamite.

"Nothing suspicious," he said.

"If that isn't the suit Nick had on, I'm blind," Teddy declared. "What are you doing around here?"

"Me come two hundred mile from Reservation. White Feather hear white man make movie picture around here. White Feather want to be in picture."

"Well, I'll be——!" Teddy scratched his head almost unbelieving. "Can you beat that, Roy?"

"Must be *two* Indians," his brother laughed. "Looks as if we'd caught the wrong fellow here."

The three looked at one another doubtfully for a moment. At length Roy broke the silence.

"Well, I suggest we escort White Feather back to the ranch. Maybe we can figure this all out there."

With the haughty chieftain between them they rode back rapidly, reaching the main gate just in time to meet Mr. Bartlett, who was coming out.

"Hello, there!" the producer called. "Success, eh?"

Roy was grinning. "We're not exactly certain whether it's success or not. This man says he is Chief White Feather. We found him on the trail heading this way. Says he was coming to get a job with you in the picture!"

Bartlett surveyed the Indian questioningly. Then he turned to Roy. "Have you looked for the dynamite?" he asked.

Roy nodded. "It's not on him, Mr. Bartlett."

The producer scanned the Indian's costume. "No, this isn't the suit I gave Nick. White Feather, eh? That your name?"

The chief nodded slowly. "White Feather want job in movie picture."

Bartlett eyed the man closely for a moment, then uttered an exclamation.

"By golly, I think I can use you, White Feather. In fact, I know I can! That is, if you boys haven't any objections to having him around for a while."

"All right with us," Roy replied. "And I guess we owe this man an apology."

"I agree," said Teddy. "By the way, how about giving White Feather the job of catching his fellow-Indian?"

The brothers broached the plan to the chieftain. After Mr. Bartlett had assured him again of a role in the picture, the man promised to spend his leisure time watching for the mysterious thief.

Nick returned at that moment, but had no further news. "I rode all the way to Dead Man's Rise," he reported. "I shore am sorry, Mr. Bartlett, 'bout that thar costume. I——"

"Never mind, Nick, it wasn't your fault," the producer replied. "We'll get it back somehow." He turned to the brothers. "Come into the house, boys. Some of my stars arrived a little while ago. I want you to meet them."

Eagerly, Roy and Teddy followed the man into the ranch-house, where Belle Ada, Nell and Curley were talking excitedly with two strangers, one a beautiful young lady, the other a kinky-haired boy of about fourteen.

"Miss Warren, this is Roy Manley and his brother Teddy," introduced the producer. "Boys, this is Billy Dixon. Miss Warren and Master Dixon are going to be the stars in our 'Sagebrush Mystery'."

"Welcome to X Bar X!" Teddy burst out, while Miss Warren smiled shyly and Billy Dixon grinned from ear to ear.

"Thank you for your welcome," said the young lady in a soft, musical voice. "This is the first time I have ever been on a ranch, and I—I'm afraid I'm a little nervous about it." Her sparkling teeth flashed as she laughed.

"Don't worry, Miss Warren, I'll take care of you!" Billy interjected manfully. "Are there any Indians around, fellows?"

"One or two, at the most," Roy chuckled, winking at his brother. "I think you'll not be bothered much, Miss Warren. Ranch life isn't as dangerous as city people think."

"Maybe Billy and Miss Warren would like to look around," Ted suggested.

At this the young lad jumped up eagerly. "I'd love to, fellows. We didn't see much of it coming in."

Miss Warren decided not to accompany them, so the brothers, with Billy chattering excitedly between them, started on a tour of inspection around the ranch buildings.

"Gee willigers, I never thought I'd see a real, honest-to-goodness ranch this size!" the young star exclaimed every few moments.

The Manleys liked the lad immensely and were looking forward to seeing him act in the picture. For the time being they refrained from plying him with the question they were eager to ask. Suddenly, as they were looking over the broad expanse behind the bunk-house, Billy became silent.

"Something wrong?" Roy queried.

"I was just thinking what a wonderful life you fellows have here with your family and all this ranch and——"

Tears welled up in his eyes, but he brushed them away with an angry gesture.

"Sorry, fellows, I—I just couldn't help thinking about something."

"About what, Billy?" Teddy asked quietly.

"Well, you probably think I'm lucky, just because I'm in the movies and all that."

Roy studied the lad's handsome face. "You certainly should be proud of yourself. There aren't many boys your age who have the chance."

"But you fellows have a dad and a mother!" The boy looked away from them as he spoke.

"You—haven't?" Teddy turned to his young friend sympathetically, while Billy slowly shook his head.

"My mother died a long time ago and my father ran away from me. Before that, he was very cruel and used to whip me every day."

"What did you do after your father left?" Roy asked hesitantly.

"Mr. and Mrs. Wilson adopted me. They've always been very kind," the young lad explained. "They brought Miss Warren and me here to-day, but are staying in Eagles at an hotel. But my father—I'm afraid he might come too."

"Your father?" Teddy exclaimed. "I thought you said he had run away years ago."

Billy looked at the brothers pleadingly. "He did, but we're afraid he'll find out where I am. He might even kidnap me because of the money I'm getting in the movies." The youngster fought manfully to keep back the tears.

"Never mind, Billy, nobody will come after you while

you're here. You may stay as long as you want to," Roy declared.

"Who was your father, Billy? What did he look like? Do you remember him? We'll keep a watch for him."

For a moment Billy was silent. Then he spoke. "He was a very ugly, thin man with only one arm. People called him One-Arm Kosty."

Chapter VII

A FIGHT

"What's the matter, fellows?" Billy exclaimed, seeing the astonishment on his friends' faces.

Roy forced a laugh. "Oh, nothing, Billy. Come on. It's time for supper."

"We haven't shown Billy the corral yet," added Teddy, taking his brother's hint. "Can you ride horse-back?"

"Shore he kin," boomed a hearty voice just then. Nick Looker came over to them from the pump.

"Hello, Nick," Teddy greeted. "This is Master Billy Dixon. He's going to be the star in the picture. Billy, this is Nick Looker, the best cowboy in the country."

"In the world, y' mean," Nick chuckled. "Glad to meet you, Billy. How 'bout a ride one o' these days?"

"Any time you say," exclaimed the young actor, who was once more his cheerful self.

"First thing to-morrow. It's time for chow now," Roy decided.

Nick, who was always eager to introduce strangers to their first horseback ride at X Bar X, looked disappointed, but waved gaily.

"O.K., fellows, but don't forget, Billy. Daybreak to-morrow we'll ride a little fence."

As soon as dinner was over, Roy took his brother by the arm.

"Let's go outside," he whispered.

Teddy nodded. "Will you excuse us, everybody? Roy and I have a little matter to attend to."

Out on the front porch the older Manley boy frowned. "I think we'd better keep our eyes doubly open now, don't you, Ted?"

His brother nodded. "Jumping coyotes, can you imagine a half-baked weasel like Kosty being the father of Billy? Golly!"

"It's a strange one, I'll tell a maverick! You know, Ted, I think we ought to ride over to Z II and check up on Kosty to-night."

"To-night? All right, I'm game."

No sooner was this decided than they made for the corral and saddled their horses.

"Goin' for a moonlight sail, boys?" queried Pop Burns, observing them from the bunk-house doorway.

"Since when have you turned sea-dog, Pop?" Roy chuckled. "We'll be back before morning, I hope."

Leaving the grizzled cowboy staring in wonderment after them, they galloped off into the glowing sunset.

"We'd better take the Crooked Gulch trail," Teddy remarked. "It's pretty rough, but it's the shortest one."

"Right. We should make it in ten hours. Ten o'clock."

Darkness gradually crept over the rocky, uneven trail, necessitating the use of flashlights to prevent Star and Flash from stumbling. At length, Roy, who was in the lead, pulled up and pointed his beam toward a large, grotesque-looking cottonwood tree.

"We're just about there now."

"Then we'd better put out the lights."

Gently they urged on their horses, proceeding slowly to avoid making any unnecessary noise. A quarter of an hour later fragments of light could be seen filtering through the trees ahead. As they moved around a bend in the trail they could see that the glow came from a single window in the midst of a group of long, rambling buildings.

"That's the bunk-house," Teddy whispered.

"You're right. Mrs. Slater is in New York now. The ranch-house is closed for the season."

"Listen!"

Faintly the sound of guitar music and harmonising voices filled the air.

"Song-fest," whispered Roy. "That's good. Now all the hands will be in one spot. Let's tie Star and Flash here and skirt around behind the bunk-house."

With their horses securely hitched to a stump near by, the boys crept noiselessly around the rim of the clearing where the ranch buildings stood. Then they advanced cautiously toward the bunk-house, whose lighted window loomed like a beacon. The sounds of singing grew louder. A moment later the boys found themselves at the rear of the rambling one-story structure.

"Take a look in the window, Roy. I'll stand watch." Teddy's voice was tense.

Roy stepped to the lighted pane and peered inside. Then he motioned to his brother.

"Looks as if Kosty is sound asleep," the older Manley chuckled.

"Guess he can't sing and feels left out," his brother laughed silently.

Together, the X Bar X boys watched the motionless

figure of One-Arm Kosty sprawled on an iron cot, the rays of a kerosene lamp flickering over his twisted face. Framed in a doorway at the opposite side of the room was a group of cowhands. One of their number was strumming a guitar. All were singing lustily:

> "Oh, I'll no more see my Sally,
> When I ride down in the valley.
> Though the sun is shinin'
> I'm a-goin' to be pinin'
> 'Cause the sun ain't shinin' for Sally.

> "Oh, my Sally's cold and dead,
> Since a c'yote bit her on the head.
> Now the trail is long
> And I cain't sing my song
> 'Cause the sun ain't shinin' for Sally.

> "Oh, I'm lonely as——"

The song suddenly ceased in a jumble of voices.

"Whar y' been, Callahan?" boomed one of the group whom the boys could not see clearly in the shadowed doorway.

"Yeah, what's the idee?" queried another. "You know we cain't do any real singin' without that thar golden voice o' your'n."

"Gold, or tin?" chimed in a third. Amid a general chorus of cat-calls and raillery a heavy-set, shifty-eyed fellow stepped into the room and put what resembled a large bundle of clothing on a table. Then he stalked over to Kosty and shook the sleeping form.

"Come on, wake up, One-Arm," he growled.

"What's th' matter?" asked the other.

As the singing commenced again, the newcomer whirled around toward the doorway.

"Cut out the racket, you waddies, I got business to talk over."

"Nothin' like leavin' when you ain't wanted," remarked a voice from the group. "C'mon, Pete, bring thet harp o' your'n over't the corral. We'll sing to the horses."

There was a shuffle of footsteps as the cowpunchers moved off. Meanwhile, One-Arm Kosty's voice was audible through the window-pane.

"What's the idea o' wakin' me up?" he was growling at the stranger.

"Look what I got!" The man whom the other cowboys had called Callahan picked up his bundle and unrolled it, deftly seizing a round white object from within the folds as he did so.

"The Indian costume!" Roy gasped under his breath.

"That's not the half of it. Look at the stick of dynamite!" his brother whispered.

Kosty was blinking uncertainly. "What in the name o'——?"

Callahan laughed hoarsely. "S'prise, eh? Well, what're you goin' to give me fer it?"

"*Give* ya? Fer what?"

"Fer this here Injun suit and the dynamite. Cain't you see it? You blind er jest asleep?"

The ugly caretaker suddenly jumped up. "Look here, Callahan, what's this? What're you talkin' about, anyhow?"

His companion chuckled unpleasantly. "Wal, I

thought the idea was to bust up things at X Bar X so's that movie fellow moves over here and we get the money fer him makin' the picture at Z II instead o' X Bar X. So I take plenty o' risk and git away with this stuff, and you set there and look dumb."

"Sure, the idea is to bust things up at the X Bar X, but I ain't made any promises about payin' people fer doin' it, least of all *you*," Kosty scowled at the other, who glared back.

"Look here, One-Arm. I got this stuff and ruined 'em over there, and either you hand over one hundred bucks right here and now or I'll——"

"You'll *what?*"

Before Callahan could move a muscle Kosty flung out a bony fist that found the squat man's chin an easy mark. With a yell he collapsed, the caretaker standing over him menacingly. For an instant neither of them moved. Then Callahan sprang at Kosty's legs, bringing the man to the floor with a crash. Excitedly, the brothers watched the ensuing struggle, but not for long.

"Teddy, now's our chance. You grab the stuff while I tell those fellows a thing or two."

When they rushed inside, Roy promptly seized Callahan's short, stubby neck and yanked him away from the caretaker, who was rapidly getting the worst of the encounter.

"Who in the name o'—who are *you?*" demanded the bull-necked fellow, struggling to his feet.

"Never mind who I am, Callahan," said Roy coolly. "But I'm going to tell you——"

"That's Roy Manley. His old man runs the X Bar X," snarled One-Arm from the floor, where he lay breathing heavily.

"Look here, you two," snapped Roy. "I'm just warning you—keep away from X Bar X or there's going to be trouble and plenty of it."

"Trouble! From you?" Callahan burst into laughter. "Why, you young upstart——"

He stretched forth two massive paws in a clumsy attempt to seize the older Manley lad by the neck. At the same instant a fist shot through the air and the fellow crumpled with a roar of pain.

"That'll fix *him*," chuckled Teddy, who had been standing by, all but unobserved. "Come on, Roy, let's move before the gang outside hears the rumpus."

Before they could retreat there came a second roar. Kosty sprang to his feet, six-shooter in hand. Like a flash, Roy dived at the ugly caretaker and the gun went flying across the room.

"Come on, Ted!"

The boys leaped outside and dodged a rain of bullets.

"Got everything, Ted?" Roy whispered hoarsely as the two ran toward the clearing.

"Yes. Hope the——"

A second blast of gun-fire mingled with shouts and yells drowned out his words.

"Horse—over to left," panted Roy as the boys tried desperately to get their bearings in the blackness.

A gun was blazing forth somewhere behind them, as the hoarse shouts of their pursuers grew louder.

"Sounds as if—whole army—behind." Teddy, breathing hard, still retained his sense of humour.

Just as they were ready to drop from exhaustion, Roy uttered a cry. They had run headlong into Star and Flash. In a twinkling the brothers were in the saddle.

"We'd better take the old trail, Ted. They're sure to come after us if we follow the regular one."

Precious moments were lost as they searched for the obscure beginnings of a trail formerly used, but long since overgrown with sagebrush and thicket.

"Here it is, Ted."

The older lad snapped on his flashlight long enough to identify a gnarled tree. A moment later they were flying dangerously over the rocky path in a desperate effort to put as much distance between themselves and their pursuers as possible.

At length, Roy reined up. "Hear anything?"

"Not a sound. Golly, that was a close call. I was just waiting for one of those bullets to smack this stick of dyn—— Say, where is it?" With an exclamation Teddy jumped to the ground and unrolled the bundle under his arm.

"Jumping coyotes, Roy, I *had* it! It was wrapped up in the costume and must have fallen out while we were riding."

"Well, it'd be silly to look for it now. No telling when we'd bump into somebody. Too bad."

Disconsolately, Teddy swung his light to and fro over the costume and the ground adjacent.

"Wouldn't that make you—— Listen! Am I hearing things?"

"I'll say you are. Those fellows must have split up and taken both trails. Come on!"

Faint sounds of hoof-beats and shouting far back on the trail were growing louder rapidly. Wrapping up the costume, Teddy jumped back on Star and once more they galloped off, riding steadily for two hours. After what seemed an eternity, lights twinkled ahead. When they reached home a few minutes later, Nick Looker strolled out from the bunk-house to meet them.

"Where in the name o' Mike have ye been?" The cowboy's flashlight beam came to rest on Roy's shirt. "Jumpin' prairie dogs, lad, ye're bleedin' to death!"

Chapter VIII

KIDNAPPED!

As the others hurried to his side, Roy gazed wonderingly at his shirt.

"Shucks, it's only a scratch, boys. Some brambles, probably. We were riding pretty fast."

"Brambles nothin'," Nick snorted. "Get off that horse and make it quick. Ted, go call your dad."

Roy suddenly turned pale and felt his knees give way under him. An instant later all went black before his eyes.

"What's happened?" called a voice in the darkness, as Mr. Manley appeared with Ted.

"Roy fainted, Mr. Manley." The cowboy was loosening the boy's clothing. "Let's carry him inside."

A few moments later Roy lay with his chest bared under a strong light while his father made a careful examination.

"A bullet, you say?"

"Probably, Dad," replied the younger Manley, who had given his father a quick recital of the evening's happenings. "They fired at us."

"He's comin' to," announced Nick suddenly. He put down a bottle of spirits of ammonia which he was holding as Roy's eyelids opened slowly.

"Where—where am I? Hello, what's going on here, anyhow?"

"Just hold your horses, son." Mr. Manley worked

deftly with his emergency surgical kit. "There! See it?" He straightened up and held out a tiny object.

"Bullet, eh?" Nick stared incredulously.

"It was probably just about spent when it clipped him," Mr. Manley explained. "I found it under his skin. Here, Ted, slap on this bandage. You'll be all right by morning, Roy."

Skilfully, Teddy applied the bandage and tucked his brother under a blanket.

"Now, boys," said their father, "we'll grab a little sleep. Then I want to hear all about this escapade first thing in the morning."

At breakfast, Hamilton Bartlett listened tensely. Roy, except for a slight pain at the site of his injury, was feeling like himself again, and recounted their experience of the night before.

"Amazing! Amazing!" repeated the producer with a scowl when Teddy had finished. He drummed his fingers on the table meditatively. "Manley," he went on, "I don't know what this is all about, but I think I'd better get in touch with the owner of that ranch. What's her name?"

"Slater. Mrs. Slater. Mightn't be a bad idea, Bartlett. Wait a minute, I'll look up her address in New York. Teddy——"

"I'll get it, Dad." His younger son hastened to his father's study and returned with an address book.

"The boys can ride to Eagles with it if you want to send a wire, Bartlett," the ranch owner suggested.

The man's eyes twinkled. "Sorry, Manley, one of your men will have to do it. Your sons are in the movies now, and we've work to do this morning!"

The brothers needed no urging. While the producer

composed a telegram to the rich widow who owned Z II, they set about placing the heavy movie cameras at strategic points near the corral. Bartlett joined them a short while later.

"The rest of my company should be here to-day, boys, but in the meantime I want to shoot some more riding. Go ahead and saddle up."

A throng of ranch hands and cowpunchers already had gathered, many of them from neighbouring places, so that the scene resembled a gala festival. Shortly before noon one of the wagons returned from Eagles filled with strangers. As it drew up alongside the crowd, Bartlett motioned to Roy and Teddy, who had just completed an hour's riding in front of the cameras.

"Want you to meet the rest of the gang, fellows," he called. For the next thirty minutes the ranch-house was a steady hum of voices as the newcomers were introduced to the Manley family and to Nell and Curley, who had just ridden over with Mr. Ball, genial owner of 8 X 8.

"All right, everybody, no time to waste," announced the producer impatiently when greetings had been exchanged all around. "Slim, you and Joe get out to the cameras. Miss Warren, are you ready for Scene Four? We're going to shoot that one now. Seabury, Nick, here, will take you to our improvised dressing-room in the bunk-house. Come on, Roy and Ted, I'll need you for some more riding."

At Mrs. Manley's insistence, Bartlett was persuaded to give himself and his cast time out for a hasty luncheon, following which all hands went back on location at the corral.

"Where's White Feather?" the producer grumbled, gazing around at the crowd about him.

"White Feather ready," boomed a voice, as the chieftain stepped out regally from the crowd of on-lookers.

"Good. I thought you were out scalping somebody," said Bartlett with an ironic smile. "All right, let's have it quiet while I explain the action. Everybody got a script? Turn to page——"

Suddenly a wild shriek from the direction of the ranch-house kitchen interrupted everything. Norine came flying out.

"Robbers! Robbers in the house! Mr. Manley!"

Several cowboys dashed up to the kitchen door in time to meet a tall, fierce-looking individual, heavily bewhiskered, and carrying a long-barrelled revolver in either fist.

"Tackle 'im, Pete!" yelled Pop Burns, detaching himself from the crowd and rushing toward the knot of cowpunchers surrounding the stranger. A roar went up as every man in the throng made for the spot.

"Hold on!" came a yell louder than the rest. "Leave him alone. That's Joel Seabury!" Bartlett tried frantically to push his way into the crush around the stranger, who by now had disappeared somewhere underfoot. "Get away from him, men! He's my villain!"

When the confusion subsided a moment later, a battered, dishevelled fellow with half his moustache ripped off struggled to his feet. Instantly Mr. Manley was at his side.

"Hurt, Mr. Seabury? I'm certainly sorry. Come into the house."

The other smiled sheepishly. "I'm all right, thanks.

Didn't think my make-up was going to be as effective as all that!"

The cowboys broke into mumbled apologies.

"Shore thought a maniac'd got loose," Pop Burns said guiltily. "Sorry, Mr. Seabury. The men here ain't used to make-believe villains."

The actor looked at his audience and suddenly burst out laughing. With the tension thus broken, everybody joined in. Even Nick, whose affection for the cook's young daughter had swiftly turned to anger at the supposed robber, finally decided to smile.

"All right, fun's over," said Bartlett at length. "Joel, go fix your make-up."

Half an hour later the set was ready once more. Bartlett outlined the action that was to take place and gave the signal for his assistants, Slim and Joe, to grind away at the cameras. Most of the acting planned for Roy and Teddy at the moment consisted of riding feats, which they performed to the admiration even of the seasoned cowboys among the spectators.

"You ought to be proud of those sons of yours, Manley," Mr. Ball remarked as he and his fellow ranchmen stood watching.

"Shore he should. I ain't seen better ridin' in the whole West," was the emphatic agreement of a grizzled veteran of the range standing near by.

Mr. Ball nudged Bardwell Manley, and smiled. "You're ruining my ranch, Manley. All my hands are spending their time over here. That's my foreman. Oh, here comes your cook."

A squat figure elbowed his way through the crowd to the owner of X Bar X.

"Missee Manley, teleglam for Missee Baltlett. Gussee bling flom Eagles."

"Oh, much obliged, Sing Lung. Bartlett! Can you come here a minute?"

The producer announced a rest period, then hurried over. "Let's go inside and read it, Manley," he said under his breath. "Oh, Nick, tell Roy and Teddy to come into the house, will you?"

A few moments later the boys and their father drew up chairs, waiting while Bartlett scanned the message. At length he cleared his throat.

"Well, we all knew there was dirty work afoot over there at Z II, and there *is*. Listen to this from Mrs. Slater: *My caretaker reported you were using Z II for movie production Stop I authorised substantial increase in wages for all hands accordingly Stop Surprised to know situation as you wired me Stop Have ordered Lawyer Eppirt at Eagles to dismiss men hire others.* Well, what do you think of that?"

"I'm not surprised at anything One-Arm Kosty might have engineered," Roy muttered.

"Well, that's that," remarked Mr. Manley. "I guess we'll have no more trouble from that quarter."

"I'm not so sure, Dad," Teddy said, frowning. "Kosty won't thank anybody for being fired, and neither will Callahan and the rest of the men."

"You're right," agreed his brother. "We'll have to keep on our toes for certain now."

Suddenly the door of Mr. Manley's study burst open. Nat Sell, red-faced and perspiring, rushed in.

"Stampede, Mr. Manley! Shelter Valley!" Turning on his boot heel, the cowboy rushed out again. The four in the room looked at one another for an instant, then leaped to their feet almost simul-taneously.

"We'll go right down, Dad. See you later," Roy called back over his shoulder as he and Teddy raced toward the corral, from which riders were departing as fast as they could saddle their mounts. In a jiffy the brothers joined them.

"Shelter Valley is where Mr. Ball's ranch joins ours," Roy said tensely as the boys galloped full-tilt over the prairie.

"That gives me an idea," muttered Ted. "I noticed a whole gang of 8 X 8 men over here this morning watching the work on the picture."

"What's that got to do with the stampede?"

"I'll bet my shirt Kosty and his gang knew the ranch was just about deserted and——"

"Took advantage of the fact to cause a stampede of Mr. Ball's cattle! Golly, I'll bet that's the answer. You'll be a professional detective yet," he chuckled. "Great Scott, look!"

A huge cloud of dust swept toward them over the horizon, while a chorus of shouts and yells went up from the galloping cavalcade of cowboys from X Bar X.

"The cattle are heading toward us!"

"Us? They'll be in the ranch-house in ten minutes!"

"Somebody go back and warn the women!"

The stentorian voice of Pop Burns boomed above the uproar. "Gus! Go back and tell 'em at the ranch the stampede's headed their way. Rad, you and Jim Casey stay here. If the rest of us cain't bust up them critters before they get this far, mebbe you can do it at this point."

The veteran foreman's orders, necessary though they

were, took up valuable time. The herd was now dangerously close, and the thunder from a thousand hoofs filled the air.

"Kiyi-yi-yi! Kiyi-yi-yi! Yippee-e-e-e!"

With all a cowboy's desperate art of breaking up a rush of maddened cattle, the men galloped full-tilt into the teeth of the stampede. Shouting and yelling, they waved their sombreros frantically. At length, bit by bit, the herd slowed down and began to scatter.

"Go after the strays!" yelled Pop Burns at Teddy as he swept past in a wide circle. Just then Roy rode up, breathing hard.

"Going after strays, Ted? Let's start down at Shelter Valley. Might be some left there."

Without pausing for breath, the brothers galloped off.

"Golly, I thought we'd be having steer for supper to-night. Boy, was that a close one!" Teddy mopped his brow with his free hand.

Roy laughed dryly. "I thought they would be having *us* for dinner!" His face grew serious. "If I could be sure Kosty had a hand in this——!"

"As far as I'm concerned, I *am* sure. You wait, Roy, we'll prove it yet."

Twenty minutes of hard riding brought the boys to a deep gorge known as Shelter Valley because of the giant cottonwood trees abounding in the vicinity. The stout fence separating 8 X 8 and X Bar X territory was as flat as if it had never stood. Dismounting, the boys hobbled Star and Flash, and went over to examine the wreckage.

"It's been cut, all right." Roy held up a strand of wire. "Clean as a whistle."

Teddy eyed the wire disgustedly. "Somebody's got to do something about all this soon. We can't be having stampedes every time we turn around!" Suddenly he looked over his shoulder and uttered a cry. "There's a dead dogie, or I'm a dodo."

They hastened to the edge of a near-by ravine from which a white object projected. It proved to be the head of a trampled steer. To their dismay nine other bodies lay strewn about the vicinity.

"There go a thousand dollars of Mr. Ball's money, and Kosty's going to pay it back," Teddy snapped. "I intend to——"

"Look!"

Roy pointed at the soft earth near the spot where they were standing.

"That's not a steer track," he said, "nor a horse's, either. Looks like a big dog's."

Excitedly, the boys studied the strange imprint in the mud.

"Here are some more," exclaimed Teddy. "What do you suppose——?"

"Either some timber wolves got into the cattle and started the stampede, or One-Arm Kosty planted them here for the purpose."

"Just what I was thinking. I don't know whether they're timber-wolf tracks or not, but they don't belong around here. No timber wolves in this vicinity."

Still puzzling over their peculiar discovery, they decided to return home and reveal nothing for the time being.

"Don't see any strays," Teddy observed on the way back.

"Pop probably got tired of waiting for us and

rounded them up himself," Roy laughed. "Maybe he'll forgive us if we get some new wire and go back and fix the fence."

Half an hour later they reached the ranch-house, where their father met them on the front porch. Mr. Manley's face wore a puzzled look.

"Isn't Mr. Bartlett with you?"

The brothers looked at each other. "We haven't seen him, Dad," Roy said, with a feeling that something was wrong. "What's the matter?"

"He's disappeared. I thought he might be with you. All the other men and horses are accounted for. You're the last in. Nobody's seen Bartlett since the stampede started."

Chapter IX

A DANGEROUS MISSION

"Probably Mr. Bartlett went to Eagles on business, Dad. Maybe he went to see Sam Eppirt," suggested Roy, sensibly.

Mr. Manley shook his head. "I got in touch with Sam and he hasn't seen him. Besides, why would Bartlett run off in the middle of a day's work without telling anybody?"

A pleasant-faced young man appeared just then from behind the ranch-house. The boys recognised him as Slim Downey, one of the cameramen.

"Pardon me, Mr. Manley, I'm looking for Mr. Bartlett. Have you seen him?"

"Why, no," the ranchman began.

"Guess he'll be back soon," said the young man breezily. "Say, did we get some shots of that stampede! Joe and I were right in the middle of things with the cameras!"

"That's great!" Teddy exclaimed. "Here's hoping we won't have any more stampedes for a long time to come!"

"I second the motion," chirped a musical voice as a young lady, immaculately attired in a riding-habit, emerged from the house.

"Why, Miss Warren, don't tell us you were in the round-up too," Roy said, laughing.

The lovely young actress smiled. "And why shouldn't I be? Your friend Nick put me on a horse and, well, I——"

"She did some of the prettiest riding I ever filmed!" chimed in Slim Downey. "Right there in the middle of everything, and wasn't scared a bit."

"That's all you know about it," laughed Miss Warren. "The truth of the matter is, I was so frightened I didn't dare fall off!"

Mr. Manley smiled. "Young lady," he said heartily, "you rode like an old hand at the game. Too bad Bartlett wasn't here——" He bit his lip, and the actress's face suddenly became serious.

"Doesn't anybody know where he is?" she queried anxiously. "This is the first time I have ever heard of him leaving a set in the middle of a day's work."

The others were silent. At length Roy spoke up. "We think he went to Eagles on a business matter, Miss Warren. He should be back before long."

"I hope so. And now if you'll excuse me I shall go change for dinner."

She waved gaily, but it was evident she was worrying over the producer's unexplained absence. A moment later the cameraman likewise excused himself. The brothers stood wondering what their next move should be.

"There's something decidedly wrong," Roy mused. "Do you suppose——?"

"If you're thinking the same thing I'm thinking, we'd better do something pronto," Teddy burst out. "I'll bet a pair of stirrups Mr. Bartlett's been kidnapped!"

"You've guessed it, Teddy. Dad, do you mind if we do a little investigating?"

"I've already called Sheriff Wilkins, boys, but if you think we can find a clue in the meantime, go ahead."

As the two mounted their horses, Teddy queried, "What's your plan, anyhow? Are we going back to Z II?"

Roy's face was tense. "I've another idea. Remember old Cactus Tom at the general store in Eagles?"

"Remember him! Why, certainly."

"Well, if he doesn't know more about what goes on around here than anybody alive, I'll eat my bandanna. I have a strong hunch that he might have heard something or other that may give us a clue. It's just a hunch, of course."

Star was pawing the ground impatiently. "Well, maybe it's worth a try," Teddy agreed, though uncertainly. "It's a cinch we can't stand here all day. What about going over to Z II and checking up?"

Roy shook his head. "Not yet. No use borrowing trouble before we have to. If we can't find out anything from Cactus Tom we'll have plenty of time to go back to Z."

An hour's hard riding brought them to the outskirts of Eagles. A few minutes later Star and Flash were tied to the hitching-post in front of a ramshackle frame building on Main Street. The boys entered a room littered with every imaginable kind of merchandise.

"Wal, 'pon my word ef 'tain't them two coyotes from X Bar X!" cackled a greeting from the rear of the store, and a mountain of flesh partly covered with a soiled apron bore down upon them.

"Hello, Cactus," Roy exclaimed cordially, for the boys had known the huge proprietor ever since they could remember. Now he waddled up and held out a bulbous hand.

"Glad to see ye. By all the timber wolves in South

Africee, business hain't been so good sence the flood at Jester's Gorge. It's jest as One-Arm was sayin' not more'n an hour ago——"

Teddy started. "Who? One-Arm?"

"That's right, One-Arm Kosty. Ye know 'im, don't ye, lads? Wal, he says as how good luck comes all 't once and thet's jest what's happened to-day. All my old friends come in the same day!"

The fat store owner paused to get his breath, beaming at the boys.

"What's going on, anyhow? Rodeo somewhere?" Roy queried innocently.

"You ought to know, lads. Ain't some fella from Hollywood makin' movies of your outfit? Wal, all the boys has been comin' in to buy their glad rags in case the movie stars is a-goin' to look 'em over. Especially that pretty one I been hearin' 'bout." Cactus Tom threw back his head and let out a roar of laughter. Teddy winked at his brother.

"Don't tell us One-Arm's coming over all dressed up too!"

The proprietor mopped his brow. "Wal, now, come to think on't, Kosty come in to get him a new bowie knife. Said he was a-goin' out to look fer strays and might have to do some campin' nights. Say, you lads are sure lookin' fine. Brown as berries, y'are."

Roy smiled. "Thanks for the compliment, Tom. So Kosty's out looking for strays? Wonder where?"

"He didn't say. Up Cottonwood Trail way, I guess. Pete Smith was in just afore you boys and he said he saw 'im headin' thataway."

Teddy quickly changed the subject. The boys lingered a few moments longer, telling Cactus Tom of the activities at their ranch as they made a few purchases. At length they took leave of the eccentric old store owner.

"What'll it be? Cottonwood Trail?" Teddy asked, fairly bursting with excitement.

"Right. That story of looking for strays sounds a bit fishy if you ask me."

They wheeled their horses about and headed for the outskirts of the village, where a rocky path disappeared over a knoll.

"That's it," Roy decided. "Golly, I haven't ridden along Cottonwood Trail for years."

As they picked their way carefully over the rough path, the brothers secretly became more and more concerned over the possible outcome of the journey. If Kosty really had kidnapped Bartlett, what would happen? Moreover, might he not attempt the same thing with young Billy Dixon?

"Shucks," muttered Teddy after a while. "I think this is going to be a wild-goose chase. It's already growing dark."

"Maybe so," said the older boy. "At any rate, if we ride far enough we'll be back home again."

"With nothing to show for our trouble. Personally, I think we should have gone over to Z II in the first place. Say, do you smell smoke?"

The boys pulled up short. "By golly, Ted!" Roy sniffed the darkness. "Wood fire somewhere." He dropped his voice to a whisper. "We'd better stop and have a look around."

Dismounting, the boys led Star and Flash to the edge of the trail, where they hitched the two ponies to the limb of a cottonwood tree. Silently the boys stole along the trail, taking pains not to dislodge pebbles and rocks or otherwise run the risk of being heard.

"The wind's blowing our way, thank goodness," Teddy breathed.

Roy stopped suddenly. Not far ahead they could hear a faint crackling sound.

"Camp fire, sure as you're alive."

They crept around a bend. Through the thicket alongside the trail, scarcely a hundred yards away, a red glow could be seen. The figure of a man lay motionless in the flickering shadows near by.

"If he's asleep we'll make it," Roy whispered tensely. "If he's awake he'll hear us for certain."

Teddy answered by stepping on a dead branch in his path. There was a sharp report, which made the boys stand breathless. But the man did not move.

"Let's go." Roy crept into the thicket with his brother at his heels. Every few seconds a twig would snap under their feet. Still the prone figure did not move.

Suddenly Roy nudged his brother. "It's Kosty, all right," he whispered.

"Yes. Couldn't mistake *that* face."

After a quarter of an hour of precarious crawling the lads from X Bar X reached the edge of a small clearing, in the centre of which a camp fire burned merrily. Kosty was snoring.

"What's in his hand?" Teddy speculated under his breath.

"Looks like a letter."

"Shall we get it?"

"Stay here and watch. I'll try it."

Reluctantly Teddy remained in the shadows as his

brother slowly crept forward. Kosty moved. With his heart skipping beats, Roy halted, but the ugly caretaker settled down again, snoring louder than ever. Silently the boy crept on.

Only a few feet of ground now separated him from the sleeping form. Suddenly a clatter of hoof-beats resounded through the darkness beyond.

Chapter X

AN IMPORTANT LETTER

With a desperate leap Roy reached the sleeping man's side and tugged gently at the sheet of paper in his gnarled fist. It slipped out. At the same instant the snoring ceased. Then Roy dashed into the shadows as a horseman came flying into the clearing.

Kosty was rubbing his eyes. "What's the idea?" he glared at the newcomer.

"Callahan!" Teddy exclaimed under his breath. His brother, still clutching the sheet of paper, nodded.

"What's the idea o' what?" snorted the rough-looking cowboy, dismounting and flinging the foam and lather from his jacket. "Don't you ever do nothin' but sleep when I'm waitin' for you?"

"Shut up, Callahan. Why aren't you back where you're s'posed to be?"

The heavy-set fellow swaggered up and down before the fire. "Why ain't *you*? You claim to know everythin'. Why ain't you back fixin' up Bartlett?"

"Fixin' up Bartlett? What do you mean?" The caretaker scowled wolfishly. "Say, what've you been doin' since I left there, anyhow?"

Callahan stopped his pacing. "Well, it's like this. Bartlett gets tough, so I give 'im some stew with rat p'ison in it. He gets sick, an'——"

"What's that? You give Bartlett rat p'ison? You yellow-livered, locoed——"

Callahan turned on the other with a snarl. "Listen,

One-Arm, you ain't callin' me and the men no more
names. And what's more, you're a-goin' to put us wise
about a few things. What's the idea o' kidnapping
Bartlett, in the first place?"

The cowboy glared at Kosty, who squirmed uneasily.

"None o' your business. I said you'd be paid,
didn't I?"

"Rats, One-Arm," hissed the other. "Your word's no
good and we ain't a-goin' to be party to no more
mysteries. Come on, now, come clean. If you don't
you're a-goin' to find yourself with a mess o' trouble on
your dirty hands."

For a moment Kosty was silent. Then he shrugged
resignedly. "Oh, well, long's you feel thataway about it,
I'll tell you. Where's that letter?"

"What letter?"

"Wind musta blowed it away. Anyhow, it's like this.
My kid run away from home and got to be a movie
star. He's makin' big money under the name o' Billy
Dixon. I got reason to believe Bartlett can tell me
where to find 'im."

"Well, what about it? What's that got to do with me
and the men?"

One-Arm smiled evilly. "You're dumber'n I thought,
Callahan. If we find my kid I'll get hold of his salary,
natur'lly. I'm his dad, ain't I? Then I'll split with you
and the men."

Callahan began his pacing again. "Sounds pretty far-
fetched to me. Sure you ain't lyin'?" He stuck his
grizzled chin in Kosty's face. "If I thought you was
lyin'——"

"I ain't lyin', you lunkhead, but if you've killed
Bartlett we gotta start all over again."

Callahan grunted. "Aw, he's not killed, jest a little weak. Come on back and look at 'im."

While the man stamped out the fire, Kosty disappeared into the thicket, emerging a moment later with his horse. As the men disappeared, the boys sprang into action.

"You go back and bring up Star and Flash. I'll take a squint at this letter in the meantime," said Roy.

Teddy flew down the trail to the spot where their ponies were tethered, and was back with them in a jiffy. "Ready?" he called.

"Yes," was the reply.

The lad was on Star in an instant. As the two boys spurred their horses as much as they dared over the rocky trail, Teddy asked:

"What about the letter, Roy?"

"It's from some fellow I've never heard of, out in California. Pal of Kosty from the sound of it. Says just what we knew already. One-Arm's son is named Billy Dixon and he's in the movies."

The brothers rode in silence for several minutes; then Roy reined in Star.

"We better make sure we're on the right trail," he advised. Jumping off his pony, he pointed his flashlight at the ground where fresh hoof-marks appeared in the circular rays. "Yes, they're still ahead of us."

The lads rode for nearly two hours, stopping every few minutes to examine the trail for marks and straining their ears for tell-tale sounds ahead.

"Looks familiar around here," Teddy declared, as the moon came from behind a cloud. "Say, we're not far from Z II."

The words were hardly out of his mouth when the trail curved abruptly and the boys found themselves on the outskirts of a broad clearing. In the moonlight a huddle of large buildings only a few hundred yards away was revealed.

"Question is, what happened to Kosty and Callahan?" asked Roy.

The two from X Bar X sat on their horses in the shadows, studying the peaceful scene. Suddenly Teddy uttered an exclamation under his breath.

"Roy! Aren't those horses over there by the ranch-house?"

They strained their eyes in the direction the lad had indicated.

"Golly, I think they are. Hard to tell this far off. Say, do you suppose they have Mr. Bartlett in the ranch-house?" Roy queried tensely.

"Now's a good time to find out."

Dismounting and tying Flash to a tree, Teddy started across the clearing on all fours. In a moment his brother caught up with him.

"Good practice for being an earthworm," the younger lad smiled as they pulled themselves across the plain.

"I'll tell a maverick. I think, though, I feel more like a caterpillar with all the brambles and junk over me. Look, there's a light."

"Where? I don't see any."

"I thought I saw one in the middle of the house. Don't see it now."

A few minutes more of crawling brought the boys close enough to see faint rays of light from the cracks in one of the heavily boarded windows. Directly beneath the shuttered panes were two horses.

"No doubt about it now," muttered Roy.

Suddenly there could be heard a sharp, creaking sound at one end of the house. Two dim figures slipped from an invisible door and hurried toward the horses. Roy's heart leaped in his throat.

"Stay low," he whispered.

"Don't worry!" muttered Teddy dryly.

The boys were only a dozen yards from the house, with the moon shining full upon them. If the two horsemen, who were now recognisable as Kosty and Callahan, should chance to come directly toward them——

"Whew! That was a close one," breathed Roy as the ruffians galloped off in the opposite direction.

"You're right. Well, let's get to work. They may be back any minute."

"No doubt of it," his brother agreed.

Peering around to make certain no other ranch hands were about, the brothers made a dash for the house. There was no sign of the feeble light they had seen previously.

"Where do you suppose that door is, Teddy?"

"Over here some place, I think. Stand watch while I look." The younger Manley tapped gently along the dark walls. He stopped short as a faintly hollow sound answered his knock.

"Roy, I think this is it," he whispered.

"That doesn't look like a door to me. Nothing but solid wall. What about the real door over there?"

"I tried it. It's nailed shut. I think this is a secret panel of some sort. Come on, let's shove."

As something gave way, the boys went sprawling into the blackened interior of the big house.

"Ouch!" said Roy, sitting up and rubbing a lump on his head. "Guess you were right, Ted."

"Listen!"

A faint groan seemed to come from directly over them.

"Bartlett!"

Silently, Roy jumped to his feet and snapped on his flashlamp. It disclosed an immense carpeted room with a wide stairway at the opposite end. Less than a minute later the brothers had climbed stealthily to the second-floor landing. The groaning was louder than ever, but still seemed to be above them.

"More stairs back there," said Teddy. "Let's have a look in the attic."

Treading softly, they ascended to a low-ceilinged room at the top of the house. The sounds had ceased.

"Room's empty," said Roy, swinging his light to and fro. It revealed nothing but old furniture.

"Wait. There's a door. Looks like a closet."

No sooner had he spoken than the groaning commenced again. There was no doubt now as to where it came from. Teddy Manley sprang over to the door and gave the knob a sharp twist. Nothing happened.

"H-e-l-p!"

From inside came a long-drawn-out wail. At the same instant Teddy collided with the door full force. There was a splintering crash and a dull thud as the lad tumbled on to a pile of blankets.

"Mr. Bartlett!"

The two lads stared at the pale countenance of the producer, who lay huddled on the floor. His eyes were feverish, his clothes soiled and dishevelled.

"Thank Heaven!" he murmured, staring at the boys.

"Those—those skunks! Just wait till I——" He sank back, too weak to say anything more.

"Try to find some water, Teddy. Downstairs, maybe," Roy commanded.

The younger lad hesitated. "Don't you think we'd better leave while we have the chance?" he queried.

"Guess you're right, Ted. Come on, we'll carry him out."

Quickly they bore the executive to the broken panel on the first floor.

"Take a quick look outside, Teddy. If everything's quiet we'll make a dash for it."

In a moment Ted was back. "Everything looks all right," was his comment.

Picking up the weak form of Bartlett, they hastened desperately across the stretch of moonlit prairie to the thicket adjoining. Ten minutes later the producer was lashed securely to Star's sturdy back. The boys then mounted Flash, Roy holding the pony's reins.

"Well, here's hoping we don't run into those two scoundrels now," Teddy murmured through clenched teeth.

The brothers chose a short-cut trail which, though extremely rough, would enable them to reach X Bar X in half the usual time. Stopping every now and then at small streams to bathe Bartlett's feverish head, they found the producer becoming less weak. Presently lights in the ranch-house twinkled through the trees ahead of them.

"How come?" Roy wondered, looking at his wristwatch. "It's nearly four o'clock."

"Dad's probably worried. Waiting up for us."

"We'll be home in ten minutes, Mr. Bartlett," Roy

called, turning back toward the prone figure of the producer.

"Good," came the weak response.

As they drew closer Roy commenced flashing his light. "Maybe Dad or somebody'll see us."

The answer was a clatter of flying hoofs. A moment later a lone horseman came charging out of the darkness ahead.

"Thet you, Ranny?" rang out as a strong light suddenly split the gloom.

"Wal, I'll be skinned alive if it ain't you two Manleys!"

"Hello, Nick," Teddy called out, recognising the voice. "What on earth are you doing up at this hour of the night?"

Young Looker pointed his light at Star trailing behind and uttered an ejaculation.

"Mr. Bartlett! Are ye—is he—all right?"

"He will be in a minute. Is Dad up?" Roy queried.

"Shore is. Whole ranch is up. Waitin' fer you an' Ranny an' Billy."

Teddy pulled back Flash's reins. "Billy?" the brothers exclaimed together.

Nick eyed the brothers uneasily. "Ranny took Billy out for a moonlight ride. That was about eight o'clock last evenin' an' they ain't back yet!"

Chapter XI

THROWN FROM A PRECIPICE!

For an instant the three stared at one another in the weird glow of their flashlights. It was Teddy who broke the tense silence.

"It won't do any good to stand out here. We have a patient who needs care."

After dismounting, Roy took a hurried glance at Bartlett. The producer was still ghastly pale though conscious. The lad turned to Nick.

"Better ride ahead and tell Dad we're coming. Get some hot soup ready. Mr. Bartlett needs nourishment in a hurry."

"Righto." The cowboy wheeled his horse about and clattered off, the brothers meanwhile resuming the slow pace made necessary by the producer's weakened condition.

Roy's face was knotted. "Can you beat that, Ted! Billy and Ranny gone since eight o'clock!"

"Things are getting no better fast," his brother admitted. "Roy, there's only one thing to do and that's to——"

"Find Kosty and Callahan as soon as possible. Where do you suppose they went in such a hurry just before we found Mr. Bartlett?"

Had the boys known the answer to Roy's question a few hours earlier, their desperation would have been greater than ever, for the two ruffians were planning to carry their vicious plot to the limit. It was after midnight when the men dismounted in a small clearing half an hour's hard riding from Z II.

"Light up a fire, Kosty," snarled Callahan. "We got plenty of talkin' to do."

"Don't know why we have to go campin' out every time you want to talk," replied One-Arm sourly, peering around under his light for firewood.

"Jest as well the men don't know too much about what's goin' on, ain't it? You never know who's pokin' around the ranch-house. Now, what're we goin' to do with Bartlett?"

"Hold 'im fer ransom, just like I said. That'll bust up the movie at X Bar X and I'll get my kid back in the bargain. Look, here's the whole idee."

The one-armed man squatted by the fire and began talking to the other in a low tone. As he spoke a cruel smile gradually spread over Callahan's coarse features.

"Well," said the latter when Kosty had finished speaking, "that sounds good fer you, anyhow. But what about that guy? S'posin' he don't live through that rat p'ison? Mebbe we better have another look at 'im, eh?"

Kosty looked disgusted. "Why don't you quit yer worryin'? Didn't we look at 'im not more'n an hour ago?"

The heavy-set cowboy climbed to his feet. "Just the same, it don't pay to take no chances. You wait here, One-Arm, while I go back fer a check-up."

In a moment he had jumped on his horse and galloped off into the darkness. Kosty sat still, his thin, ugly face silhouetted against the fire. "Half-wit," he muttered aloud to himself. "How'm I goin' to get rid of 'im, anyhow?"

For a long time he sat motionless, growling curses

and threats against Callahan. Then the thump of hoof-beats resounded in the thicket, followed shortly by the big cowboy astride his mare. The man's face was twisted into a horrible scowl.

"Well, what's eatin' you this time?" mumbled the caretaker. "Scared o' the dark?"

Callahan jumped from his horse and strode over to where Kosty was sitting by the fire.

"You double-crosser!" he roared. "Try to make a simp out o' me, will you? Get Bartlett stole away so's you won't have to pay me none o' the ransom money, eh?"

The listener's jaw dropped in astonishment. Before he could say a word a huge fist had shot out and the one-armed caretaker crumpled without a sound to the ground.

Callahan glowered at the motionless figure. "I guess that'll teach *you* who you're meddlin' with!" He turned abruptly and swung himself into the saddle. "Giddap, Joe," he clucked to the animal. "Let's head over Crooked Run trail and find us a good place to sleep where we won't smell no rats."

Half a mile away two figures, one large and one considerably smaller, stood on a moon-bathed cliff. Behind them two horses were grazing peacefully.

"That's—that's the most wonderful sight I ever saw, Ranny!" came in youthful tones.

"Isn't anythin' more beautiful than the sagebrush in yonder valley when the moon's ridin' high, son," commented a second voice in rich, mellow tones. There was an interval of silence, then, "Glad you came, Billy?"

"Am I! I wouldn't have missed this for anything,

Ranny. Everybody at the ranch says you're a wonderful singer. Will you, I mean, would you mind singing me a song now? A real cowboy song?"

Ranny laughed softly and patted the young lad's tousled head. "Billy, I'd do anythin' for you. Just wait till I think up somethin' you'll like. Let's see, now——"

There was a slight rustling in the thicket near by. Billy started, then chuckled.

"I thought I heard something, but I guess it was only the horses. Gosh, it's lonely out here, isn't it, Ranny? But I like it."

"I know a song for you, Billy," Ranny exclaimed.

The clear voice of the cowboy floated plaintively over the calm night air, drowning out the strange rustling sound which had commenced again in the thicket:

> "I kin ride fence all day
> Always carefree and gay,
> Whoopee-ti-addy-ti-yo.
> I kin rope a lone steer
> And brand him without fear,
> Whoopee-ti-addy-ti-yo."

Billy's eyes shone with delight. "That's wonderful, Ranny. That's——"

"Whoa, there, old pal, that's not all. Listen to this:

> "I kin sing in the night
> To sagebrush and moon——"

"LOOK OUT, RANNY!"

Billy let out a sharp scream as a hulking shadow leaped past him from the bushes and collided with the cowboy on the brink of the precipice. Ranny disappeared without a sound. Before the lad could move, the mysterious figure turned and hurtled toward him.

"Help! Ranny, where are you? Ran——!"

The boy's shrieks were choked off by a large bandanna thrust into his mouth. An instant later he was dragged into the thicket. Then the moon disappeared behind a cloud, making the night very dark.

"Shucks," Teddy was complaining. "First the moon nearly shows us up when we're trying to keep ourselves under cover, and now it's gone and you can't see your hand before your face."

"Well, that's life," Roy laughed mirthlessly. "We haven't far to go before we'll be back at Z II."

"Thank goodness for Star and Flash. They're just about as sure-footed at night as they are in the daytime. What are we going to do, though, if we can't find Kosty and Callahan at Z II?"

"Take the trail they followed while we were watching them, before we located Mr. Bartlett."

Teddy scratched his head. "Sounds easy, if there's only one in the direction they went. We couldn't see much of them after they'd gone about ten feet."

"I think I remember a path leading from the edge of the clearing where they were headed, Teddy. Anyhow, we'll soon find out."

The sudden crack of a pistol-shot split the night air. As the boys reined up in alarm a second report followed, then a third.

"It's over there, Roy!"

"No, I think it's more to the left, by that cliff. Listen!"

A faint cry came from the direction Roy had indicated.

"Is that——?"

"It's Ranny, or I'm deaf as the ranch-house gate," the younger Manley lad exclaimed. "And you're right, he's over there by that cliff some place. Come on!"

The precipice in question towered above a dense mass of sagebrush not far from the trail over which the boys had been riding. They decided to tie their horses and proceed on foot. Together they plunged into the undergrowth, their flashlights blazing.

"H-e-l-p!" rang out the weird cry, this time considerably stronger.

"It's Ranny, Ted. *WE'RE COMING, RANNY!*" the older Manley shouted back through cupped hands.

"H-u-r-r-y!"

Ten minutes of frantic scrambling through the snarled sagebrush brought them to the base of a rocky promontory. Roy pointed his light upon its steep face.

"There he is!" Roy cried.

The powerful rays came to a focus on the figure of the cowboy dangling precariously from a tiny ledge far up the side of the cliff.

"We're coming, Ranny. Can you hold on a few minutes?" Teddy called.

"I'll—try to," came a gasp. It was evident that the cowboy rapidly was growing weaker. Furthermore, a drop would mean certain destruction on the rocks below. Rapidly the brothers surveyed the desperate situation. "We can't lower a rope from the top," Roy decided. "Takes too long to get there. We'll have to climb."

"I'm afraid you're right. Well, let's go. Plenty of ledges jutting out, so we shouldn't have much trouble. HOLD ON, RANNY!"

With Roy in the lead, the brothers commenced the dangerous ascent, aided only by small shelves of rock at intervals, with here and there a sprig of scrub oak jutting out. Bit by bit they climbed, stopping every few seconds to catch their breaths and to shine their flash-lights ahead.

"Fifty feet to go, Ted," Roy gauged after they had been struggling for some ten minutes. "Are you all right, Ranny?"

"Y-y-yes," came a feeble answer.

As the boys clung precariously to a ledge, Teddy nudged his brother. "He must have a broken arm. Look how it's dangling."

Roy nodded grimly as he reached for a stout-looking shrub projecting from a crevice above their heads. As he was about to swing himself to the next higher ledge there came a terrifying snap.

"Look out!" yelled Teddy.

It was too late. Roy pitched directly into his brother and the two boys plunged into the blackness below!

Chapter XII

WHITE FEATHER WON'T TELL

Wildly Roy flung out his arms. His fingers grazed something solid. With a desperate effort he caught hold of it. Regaining his breath in a moment, he discovered that miraculously he had grasped a large branch of scrub oak.

"Ted! Ted! Where are you?"

Somewhere below him was the sound of footsteps scrambling over the rocks.

"I'm not sure where I am, Roy. How about you?"

Roy fumbled about with his feet and at length found a ledge. There he clung in the darkness, not daring to move.

"Ted, have you still got your flashlight?"

"Still have it, if it only works."

A second later the older boy's precarious landing place was bathed in brightness. With a shudder he looked down at the sharp rocks on which he surely would have landed had not the limb broken his fall.

"Better climb down, Roy. We'll start over again."

Teddy swung the light on up to the spot where Ranny had been. Grimly the cowboy was still hanging on.

"Are you all right?" the boy called anxiously.

The brothers were horror-stricken as Ranny's white fist, barely perceptible in the distant rays of Teddy's flash, began to slip. Without a second's hesitation the younger Manley was on his way up again, throwing all caution to the winds in a last desperate attempt to save the cowboy from the terrible fate awaiting him.

Roy watched breathlessly as his brother pulled himself from ledge to ledge. Fifty feet to go—forty— twenty—now Teddy was clinging to a jutting rock alongside Ranny. The Manley boy passed his arm about the man's waist just as the cowboy suddenly let go and fainted away.

"Roy, is your light working?" Teddy called.

"No. Bulb is smashed, worse luck."

Roy, having succeeded finally in working his way to the ground, was now waiting for developments above.

"I'll send mine down on my lasso," said Teddy, "I'll have to do the same thing with Ranny."

A few moments later the flashlight tinkled along the rocky face of the cliff.

"O.K., Roy, shine 'er up," the boy sang out.

Detaching the precious light from the lariat, his brother focused the beam on the pair above. Teddy already was fastening one end of the rope around Ranny's limp body, which at the same time he was forced to support with one arm. At length, satisfied that the improvised body-sling would hold, the younger Manley lad passed the coil around a heavy branch as a pulley. Then began the dangerous task of lowering the limp form. Would the device hold?

"Wait a minute, Teddy. I'd better come up and help ease him down. That'll take some of the weight off the branch," called Roy.

As quickly as possible the lad pulled himself to a point where he could grasp Ranny's legs.

"All ready, Ted. Take it easy."

Bracing himself, the younger lad slowly paid out the

lariat. Ranny, partly supported by Roy who was just beneath him, gently sank down along the face of the cliff. Thirty minutes later the boy uttered a triumphant shout.

"We're down, Ted! Come on yourself, but for goodness' sake be careful!"

By the time the other had reached the ground Ranny had recovered consciousness, and Roy was bathing his wounds in water from a near-by creek.

"Don't waste any more time with me, boys," the cowboy murmured, his face blanched with pain. "Go after Billy."

"Have you any idea what happened, Ranny?" Teddy asked.

The stricken young man shook his head. "We were standing at the top. I felt somebody give me a shove. Maybe it was Billy." Ranny's eyes twinkled and he smiled faintly.

Roy straightened up. "Ted, you stay here with Ranny. Get him home if you can. I'll go out and do a little scouting."

"All right. Good luck!"

Quickly making his way through the thicket, Roy jumped astride Star. Day was breaking as he guided the faithful animal over a rough, winding trail which led to the top of the cliff.

Suddenly a horseman appeared around a bend. With a chill Roy recognised Kosty. The fellow, idling along in the same direction, apparently had not heard Roy's approach. As the Manley boy thundered up, the caretaker wheeled around with a start. Seeing Roy, he twisted his face into a scowl.

"So it's you!" he growled.

"Get off that horse, Kosty," Roy snapped. "I want to talk to you."

Fingering the six-shooter at his hip, the ugly fellow complied without a word. Roy walked over to him.

"Stay where you are," barked Kosty, whipping out the gun. "Any talkin' you want to do you can do from where y' are."

Roy sprang at the man as quickly as a set-off steel trap. Kosty, taken by surprise, crashed to the ground. As his pistol went flying, Roy picked it up.

"Get on your horse," the boy ordered. "Hurry up about it!"

Sullenly Kosty obeyed. "I thought you wanted t' talk," he whined.

"We'll do plenty of talking back at X Bar X. Don't try any funny business, either."

As Roy mounted Star he asked, "What do you know about Billy Dixon?"

"Nothin'," muttered the ruffian. "I ain't seen 'im."

Roy was silent for a few minutes as they rode along slowly, then asked, "What's the idea of pushing X Bar X cowboys off cliffs?"

Kosty looked around at Roy and blinked. "Pushin' what off what? What're you talkin' about?"

"You know what I'm talking about. Didn't you push Ranny over a cliff last night?"

"Say, this is a frame-up," spluttered the other. "I never pushed nobody off no cliff!"

At that moment two riders appeared in the morning mist over the trail ahead, their horses proceeding at a slow walk.

"Step on it a little, Kosty," Roy ordered.

As they overtook the horsemen, they found them to be Teddy and Ranny.

"So you got our man," the younger lad observed.

Roy turned to the cowboy from X Bar X. "Ranny," he said thoughtfully, his mouth grim, "I think Kosty owes you an apology."

One-Arm glared at the others. "I never pushed him off no cliff and he knows it."

"Well, then, if you didn't do it, who did?" Roy demanded, confronting the sullen fellow and looking him straight in the eye. Kosty squirmed uneasily.

"I don't know nothin' 'bout——"

"Yes, you do." There was something ominous in Teddy's determined voice. The caretaker looked at his feet.

"Why'n't you ask Callahan?"

"Did Callahan do it? Stop your hedging, Kosty," snapped Roy. "If you don't, I'll——" The cowardly ruffian blanched. "All right, I'll talk," he whimpered. "Callahan did it, more'n likely. He's on the outs with me an' wouldn't stop at nothin' to get revenge. There, that's all I know 'bout it." He lapsed into a surly silence from which no amount of threatening would rouse him.

"Well, we'll take care of him when we get back to the ranch," Roy cut in at length. "First thing to do is to get Ranny to a doctor."

The words were scarcely out of his mouth when the cowboy slumped in his saddle and tumbled headlong to the ground. Jumping from their horses, the boys ran to the motionless figure in alarm. Kosty, without a second's hesitation, dug in his spurs and was off like a shot.

"Never mind, we'll catch him later," Teddy muttered

as he bent over Ranny. The cowboy's pulse was beating feebly. It was obvious that help would have to come soon.

"Nothing to do but get him to Doctor Gray at Eagles as fast as we can, Roy," said his brother.

Ranny was tied securely to Flash. The boys, on Star, began the arduous journey, leading their stricken friend.

When they came to a fork in the trail several miles ahead, Roy nudged his brother. "Suppose I go back to the ranch and get the wagon, Ted. I'll meet you at Eagles Pass."

A single look at Ranny, who was still unconscious, showed them that there was little time to lose. Teddy, bracing himself on Flash, supported the stricken cowboy with one arm as he held the reins in the other.

"See you in an hour, Roy," he called.

Meanwhile, Mr. Manley was standing on the ranch-house porch, puffing his corn-cob pipe nervously. Beside him stood an equally tall and heavily built individual with a five-pointed star pinned to his breast pocket.

"I tell you, Manley, there ain't a shred of evidence ag'in One-Arm fer as cuttin' them wires goes," he stated.

The other blew out a cloud of smoke and cleared his throat. "I can't help it, Sheriff, something's got to be done, and done quick. I think this Kosty fellow ought to be brought in, anyhow, for questioning."

The two men stood meditatively for a moment. Suddenly Sheriff Watkins broke the silence. "Say, look out there. Somebody's shore in a hurry."

A cloud of dust swirled over the horizon toward them. Several moments later the figure of a horseman could be discerned coming in their direction.

"Hum, that looks like Roy," Mr. Manley exclaimed. "Must have some news."

His son, clattering up to the porch, leaped off his pony.

"Want the wagon, Dad, quick! It's Ranny— he's——"

"Ranny? Hurt? You find Billy?" Without waiting for an answer the ranch owner whistled at a cowhand lounging near by. "Pete! Hitch up the wagon and bring 'er 'round here pronto. Well, son, what about it?" he added, turning back to Roy.

Quickly the boy explained the situation.

"There now, Watkins," interjected Mr. Manley when Roy had finished. "What do you think of all that?"

The sheriff straightened up and tapped his holster. "Guess you're right, Manley. We'll round up a posse. Can you spare some o' your men?"

"As many as you want, Watkins. Six or eight be enough?"

"I've an idea, Dad," Roy chimed in. "How about having White Feather go along? He probably knows more about the hiding-places around here than anybody else."

Sheriff Watkins eyed Roy questioningly.

"White Feather's an Indian chief," Roy hastened to explain. "He's here being filmed in the movie."

"If he's a real Injun we can use 'im," said the sheriff. "Where is he?"

Mr. Manley excused himself, to return a few minutes later with the dignified visitor, whom he introduced to Watkins. At the same time Pete rumbled around to the porch in the wagon.

"I'll see you later," Roy said hurriedly. "Teddy and

I'll join your posse, Sheriff, as soon as we take Ranny to Doctor Gray."

"Wait a minute, Roy, how're you goin' to find us?" the officer speculated. "White Feather, you know a lot of caves and trails around these parts. We're needin' your help to take us to One-Arm Kosty. You know him?"

Gravely the chieftain regarded them. "White Feather go," he announced solemnly.

"You know One-Arm Kosty?" the sheriff demanded a second time.

The Indian's face was a mask. "White Feather go," came the monotone again.

Roy studied the chieftain's face. Was it his imagination, or did White Feather know more than he would tell?

Chapter XIII

CAUGHT!

"Roy, you and Teddy meet us at Totem Canyon along about dark," said Sheriff Watkins.

"We'll be there," replied the lad, jumping into the wagon with Pete and driving off quickly.

Mr. Manley then turned to the Indian. "White Feather, if you're coming on our trek where do you suggest that we go?"

"Posse go in two groups," said the chieftain. "First group take trail to Smoky River, then take old path from big cottonwood tree at Rattlesnake Gorge. Other group take trail to Crooked Run. Come to old stump at fork. Take left-hand fork to Bit Mound, then——"

"Jumpin' catfish, he's a walkin' map!" exclaimed the sheriff admiringly. "Wait a minute, Blue Feather, till we get the men assembled."

"White Feather name," corrected the chieftain without the flicker of an eyelash.

From around the corner of the ranch-house appeared twelve cowboys led by Pop Burns.

"We're all ready, Mr. Manley," announced the elderly foreman. "Whar to? Oh, howdy, Sheriff."

"Howdy, men. Pop, you take five men with you. The chief and I'll go with the rest o' ye. Now, White Feather, give 'em the directions ag'in, will ye?"

The Indian eyed the men gravely. "White Feather go 'lone." He stood like an immense statue for a moment, then proceeded to repeat in detail his previous instructions, adding that a search should be made of Z II by one of the parties.

"Got all that straight, men?" queried the sheriff when White Feather had finished. "Remember, it ain't only Billy Dixon we're after, it's One-Arm Kosty too. Bring that waddy back, dead or alive."

"Alive, if possible," put in Mr. Manley.

"All right, men, git to your hosses, and be at Totem Canyon at dark."

The officer swung himself into his saddle while the cowboys rounded up their mounts at the corral. A few minutes later White Feather departed alone.

In the meantime Roy and Pete had met Teddy at the appointed place and now were engaged in the process of making Ranny as comfortable as possible in the wagon. Two hours later, with the brothers riding alongside on Star and Flash, Pete drew up in front of Dr. Gray's office at Eagles.

"Broken arm, brain concussion, and possible internal injuries," the physician diagnosed after a careful examination of the injured cowboy. "He'll have to stay here for a few days, boys. Nothing more you can do."

Thanking the doctor, and promising to return as soon as possible, the brothers went outside to send Pete back with the wagon and hold a hasty conference.

"Let's take the Old Mill trail, Teddy. That's about the only one White Feather didn't mention when he was sending out the posse."

"A good idea, Roy. Just the sort of trail Kosty would pick out. It hasn't been used in ten years, I'll bet."

"Maybe it's overgrown by now. Worth a try."

Deep in a canyon three miles from town the boys

came upon the marks of the old path, now all but obliterated by brush and thicket.

"Think we can get through, Roy?"

"Sure. Star and Flash wouldn't let a little sagebrush bother them. Let's go as far as the Old Mill and then cut through to the Totem Canyon trail."

Rocks and debris strewn along the path made the going difficult. It was almost noon when the brothers reached a dilapidated structure that once had been a mill.

"Golly, what do you suppose holds the thing up?" Teddy wondered. "It's just about ready to cave in."

Roy was staring at something on the ground not far from Star's forefeet. Dismounting, he picked up a small, glittering object.

"Teddy! Look here!"

"What is it? Billy's knife!"

Eagerly, they examined a small pen-knife with the name Billy Dixon engraved on its side.

Roy's voice sank to a whisper. "We'd better have a look inside the mill pronto. Maybe this is Kosty's hangout."

"Looks suspicious," his brother agreed.

Hobbling their horses, they climbed through the undergrowth to the sagging doorway and cautiously peered around inside.

"No sign that anybody has been here and gone," said Teddy.

Roy nodded disappointedly. "Let's see if there are any hoof-marks around outside."

A thorough inspection of the whole vicinity revealed nothing whatever in the way of a clue.

"Well, at least we've found his knife, Ted. That's something."

"I think we'd better get back and tell the posse about it, Roy. We'll just about make Totem Canyon at sundown, as it is."

Three hours of hard riding brought them to the edge of a deep gorge where, according to legend, a large Indian encampment once had been situated. A camp fire was burning ahead in a clearing.

"Who's a-comin'?" rang out a challenge, as Sheriff Watkins lumbered toward them. "Ho, it's the Manleys. Come right over, boys."

A dozen cowboys lounging about in the firelight greeted them. White Feather, sitting in a blanket apart from the others, gave no sign of recognition.

"Wal, boys," began the officer, "the men's all reported and nobody's found a trace o' One-Arm or Billy Dixon either. What about you two?"

Roy walked up to the fire. "We've found Billy's knife." He produced the object and the men crowded around with a chorus of exclamations.

"What do you know about that?" Sheriff Watkins said, scratching his head speculatively. "White Feather, did you see this?"

The chieftain had not moved from his position in the flickering shadows. "White Feather congratulate Manley boys," he chanted, then showed no further interest.

"Enthusiastic fellow, ain't he?" Pop Burns observed. "But far's I'm concerned, findin' that knife by the Old Mill looks bad. The kid may be murdered an' lyin' in some gully around there."

The veteran foreman had spoken aloud what most of the others had been thinking. Now the men looked at one another in silence.

"Wal, 'twon't do no good to set around here, men,"

Sheriff Watkins decided at length. "We'll just have to keep on a-huntin', and I think the best place to start now is the mill. Boys, why don't you ride back and tell your dad to send us some grub so's we can camp out to-night?"

Agreeing, the brothers set forth immediately, riding fast.

"White Feather is certainly a peculiar fellow, isn't he?" Roy remarked as the two galloped over the trail side by side.

"If he isn't holding something back I'll eat my hat. Where do you suppose he went after he sent the posse out?"

"Haven't the slightest idea, but I know where I think *we* ought to go. To Z II."

"I was thinking the same thing, Roy. Pop Burns says his party didn't investigate the ranch-house, only the other buildings."

"The ranch-house is the one that matters, if history is going to repeat itself. Tell you what, Ted, let's dress up as Indians. Then, if we do happen to bump into Callahan or Kosty, they won't know us."

"Good idea. Say, I'll bet Mr. Bartlett's make-up man would be able to fix us so Dad himself won't recognise us."

By the time the boys reached home their plans were set, and they were almost too excited to sleep. At the crack of dawn Roy hurried to the bunk-house, where the film company had improvised quarters. When spoken to, Harry Maxwell, the make-up man, rubbed his eyes.

"Fine time o' night to be hauling a fellow out of bed!" he laughed dryly. "So you want to look like Indians, sure enough?"

"Right," replied Roy. "We're sorry to have to wake you up, but we're in a hurry."

Maxwell fumbled around in a large kit in one corner of the room. "No trouble at all, fellows. Glad to help you out if I can see anything so early in the morning. Here!"

He drew out two Indian costumes and instructed the brothers how they should put them on. Then he produced a large box of grease paints and began to work.

An hour later Belle Ada, Nell and Curley, out for an early morning ride, were startled suddenly by the terrifying spectacle of two wild-looking Indians bearing down on them at full-tilt. A chorus of screams rent the air as the girls scattered over the prairie.

"Go away! Leave us alone!" shrieked Nell as one of the Indians veered directly toward her, grabbed her pony's bit, and brought them both to a slithering halt.

"Hurray, it worked," laughed the attacker, as Nell, who had covered her face with her arms, peered out.

"Don't be afraid, Nell, it's only Chief Pink Feather."

"Ted Manley!" squealed the pretty young girl. "You ought to be ashamed of yourself, frightening us all half to death!"

Belle Ada and Curley came up escorted by "Chief-Green-Feather-With-Purple-Stripes". Their first scare over, the girls enjoyed the joke immensely.

"But where on earth are you two going?" queried Belle Ada, her eyes wide with astonishment.

"Oh, we have a little errand," Teddy replied with a laugh. "It all depends on whether or not we look like real Indians."

"Well, you do," laughed Curley. "White Feather wouldn't know you from his own brother."

Nell's face suddenly grew serious. "By the way, Uncle Peter has been checking up on White Feather, just out of curiosity."

"Really? What did he find?" Roy asked eagerly.

"Something pretty bad?" asked Teddy.

"He found that the man really is a chief, one of the highest in his tribe."

"Good for him!" Teddy exclaimed. "Well, you girls had better go back and have your breakfast. We'll see you later."

Waving their sombreros, the brothers spurred their horses and galloped off toward the rising sun.

"Say, that sounds as if White Feather is all right after all, Ted," the older Manley lad commented as the boys raced through the crisp morning air.

"It certainly does. I was beginning to get a little suspicious of him."

"Well, you never can be sure. Because he's a chief doesn't mean we shouldn't keep an eye on him. I still think he knows a lot more than he's telling."

Discussing their plans for the day, the brothers rode until the buildings of Z II loomed ahead through the trees.

"Let's tie up here," Roy said, slipping to the ground and hitching Star to a tree while his brother did likewise. Then the two boys made their way through the thicket to the edge of the clearing.

"Where is everybody?" Teddy wondered. "Don't they do any work on this ranch?"

"So much the better for us if nobody's around. I think probably the ranch hands are having breakfast now, for smoke's coming out of the bunk-house chimney."

The brothers decided to make a quick dash for the ranch-house while they had the chance. A moment later they stood at the very point where they had previously broken in. A quick inspection showed that the secret panel had been repaired.

"I'm afraid that breaking in this time is going to be a noisy process," Roy commented, leaning against the panel. "The thing doesn't give the way it did before."

"Let's try one of these cellar windows," suggested Teddy.

He gave one tap with his foot. To his surprise the boards fell away, revealing a gaping window beyond.

"Golly, what luck!"

Roy stooped over and pointed his flashlight inside. Save for a large furnace and a flight of narrow stone steps in one corner, he could see nothing.

"All set?" Roy asked, crawling through the aperture and dropping to the cellar floor.

A moment later Teddy stood beside him. "Don't hear anything, do you?"

With his finger to his lips, Roy tiptoed to the foot of the stairway, where he hesitated a moment. "I thought I heard somebody talking," he whispered. "Guess it was my imagination."

"I don't hear anything. Let's go on up."

Before either of the boys could move from the spot, a door creaked somewhere above them.

"Stay where y' are!" boomed a stentorian voice, as a powerful light fell directly on Roy's upturned face.

Chapter XIV

IN TROUBLE!

Dazed by the glare of the light, Roy stood rooted to the spot. Heavy footsteps clumped down toward him and a powerful hand seized him by the shoulder.

"Wal, I'll be—look here, Sam, we got an Injun!"

"And there's another," crackled a voice, as a second light, cutting through the gloom of the cellar, came to rest on Teddy.

"Look here," Roy spluttered, when a rough fist clogged his mouth.

"Keep still, you. We'll hear from you later," rapped out the first speaker. "Bring your man along, Charley. We'll take 'em outside and look 'em over."

Once they were in the sunlight, the boys, to their surprise, recognised Sam Eppirt, the lawyer from Eagles, and Charley Reynolds, a burly ranger. The men seemed nonplussed at their discovery.

"Where'd you Indians come from?" demanded Eppirt.

"We're not Indians, Mr. Eppirt, we're the Manley boys. You know Dad, don't you?"

"Manley boys!" snorted the lawyer. "That's the best laugh I've had in a month. What do you think o' that, Charley?" He burst into a roar of merriment in which his companion joined.

"They speak pretty good English at that," Charley remarked when the laughter subsided. "Supposin' they ain't Injuns?"

"'Course they are, Charley. Tell you what. Wet a finger and see if their faces rub off."

The ranger eyed the boys dubiously for a moment. Then, with great deliberation, he stuck his forefinger into his mouth, drew it out, and approached Teddy. The brothers by this time were enjoying the situation. Charley drew his finger across the younger boy's cheek.

"Look at that, Sam! Look at it, red as that bandanna o' your'n! Painted Indians, just like I said."

Scowling, the lawyer looked from Charley's finger to the tell-tale streak across Teddy's cheek. Roy suddenly burst out laughing.

"What's the big joke, you young rapscallion?" demanded Sam heatedly. "Do you know you're liable for housebreakin'?"

"That's right, boys, don't make no difference whether you're Injuns or not, you busted in that house. What about it?"

"We didn't break anything, Mr. Eppirt, and we can explain everything if you'll give us a——" Roy began, when Charley suddenly uttered a shout.

"*Another* Injun, Sam! Look!"

A stalwart figure astride a white horse and bedecked in full head-dress was approaching them from a clump of sagebrush near by.

"White Feather," Teddy exclaimed.

"Who?" demanded Eppirt, his patience rapidly becoming exhausted.

"White Feather. He's an Indian chief staying at our ranch," the older Manley lad explained.

"I'm warnin' you, young fellow, any more o' your jokes and there's goin' to be plenty o' trouble." The lawyer fell silent as the horseman rode up and stopped before them.

"Who are you?" the lawyer said, eyeing the chieftain sceptically.

"Me White Feather."

"Say, you look like a real Injun," Charley butted in. "What about these two young fellows here? They belong to your tribe?"

The chief slowly shook his head. "They not Redskin, they white men in paint. Fool other white men."

Deliberately, Teddy walked up to the man. "You recognise us, don't you?" he asked.

The Indian nodded. "Manley boys," he intoned, gazing over their heads.

"There, isn't that proof enough, Mr. Eppirt?" Roy urged. Up to this point, the lawyer had shown signs of doubting the boys' identity.

"Wal, I guess you're Bardwell Manley's lads, all right, but that don't make it right to break into other people's ranch-houses."

"We're only doing what we can to try to locate Billy Dixon," Teddy said.

Eppirt snorted. "You'd better cut out the detective business and stick to bein' cowboys. I'll let you go this time, but I'm warnin' you to stay out o' cellars."

White Feather, who apparently had taken no notice of the conversation, now dismounted and faced the lawyer.

"White Feather want to ask question. Has death of white man, Hadley Slater, been explained?"

Eppirt looked at the Indian quizzically, then shook his head. "No, it hasn't. Why, do you know anything about it?"

"When wallet belonging to Hadley Slater be found, murder will be solved," chanted the native.

"That so?" Eppirt arched his eyebrows. "Well, now, maybe you can find it, Chief. Let me know if you do, will you?"

Without changing his expression, White Feather turned, mounted his horse, and galloped off.

"Queer bird," Charley commented. "Say, Sam, what's that Hadley Slater case about? All happened b'fore I come to these parts."

Eppirt plucked a blade of grass and stuck it between his teeth before speaking. "It was this way. Old Hadley Slater sold ten thousand head o' cattle one time for cold cash to a fellow who came all the way from Chicago to see 'em. Then suddenly Slater disappears."

"Warn't he ever found?"

"The body was, wedged in a crevice in Torture Cave in Totem Canyon. The wallet that his wife said he had the money in hasn't been seen since. Might have dropped behind some o' them rocks, and again it might not have."

Charley grunted. "Plain case o' murder, if you ask me. Otherwise, what was he doin' in the cave in the first place?"

"Wal, Slater was keen on exploring. He was always in one cave or another, so that didn't mean anything. Say——!" Suddenly he turned toward the boys, whom he had apparently forgotten for the moment. "Who told you fake Indians to hang around here? Go along! Beat it! And remember, if there's any detecting to do around here, there are regular officers o' the law to 'tend to it." The lawyer scowled darkly at them, but Roy thought he caught a twinkle in the man's eye.

A few moments later the boys were riding rapidly toward X Bar X. Mr. Manley met them on the porch of the ranch-house.

"Nothing new, eh?" he said, reading the expressions on their faces. "Well, there's no news here either. The posse looked all over the old mill and couldn't find a single clue."

Mr. Bartlett came up, appearing as fit as ever, but worried. "Hello, boys. No trace of our youngster yet?"

"No, we haven't found any evidence except that of the pen-knife," Roy replied.

"The men are still out looking, including Sam Eppirt and his rangers," said the boys' father. "In the meantime, there's nothing much we can do but wait."

Bartlett cleared his throat. "I feel very bad about all this," he said, "but work must go on. My people are being paid for their time. I see some of your ranch hands are getting ready to do a little branding. Wonder if I could get a picture of a brand being put on."

"Don't see why not. No need to wait for the regular round-up. Roy and Teddy'll rope a steer and you can go ahead right now."

"Fine. How about it, boys?"

Worried though the brothers were, they were only too eager to be of assistance to the genial producer. It was only a matter of moments before they found Nick and told him of their plan.

"Sure thing, fellows, I'll bring you the brandin' outfit in no time. Where do you want it, Mr. Bartlett?"

The producer was again a dynamo of nervous energy. "Put it over there in the corral, Nick. Harry, you set up the cameras. All right, boys, we'll be ready when you are."

Quickly word spread around the ranch that a steer was to be branded for Bartlett's benefit. A crowd of ranch hands assembled to watch the procedure. Among them was Ranny, who came out from the bunk-house on a crutch, and his left arm in a sling.

"Hi, Ranny!" Teddy called. "Feeling O.K.?"

"Not bad, considerin'," laughed the injured cowboy. "Go ahead an' do your stuff."

The brothers conferred hastily. "Ted, you run the steer in and I'll do the roping. That ought to make a good picture," Roy suggested.

"Sounds fine to me," Bartlett agreed. "Try to stay around the cameras if you can. We don't want to miss anything."

A herd of cattle was grazing not far away. Teddy jumped on Flash, singled out a steer near the edge of the group, and galloped toward the animal at full-tilt. The crowd watched breathlessly as the younger boy expertly headed the beast toward the cameras.

"Attaboy, Teddy, push 'im along!" shouted Rad Sell, whereupon a chorus of cries went up.

"Get 'im goin', Teddy!"

"Watch out, he's swervin' off!"

"Look at 'im go now, will ye? Keep clear, everybody!"

The beast charged directly for the corral. Harry, tense with excitement, was turning the handle of the camera for all he was worth.

In the meantime Roy made ready with his lariat. Gauging the distance the animal still had to cover before he should reach the corral, the lad suddenly dug his heels into Star's quivering flanks and raced out, the lasso whirling over his head.

"There he goes!" roared the onlookers. "Rope him good, Roy!"

The lariat snaked through the air. For a breathless instant the steer charged on, then suddenly reared up on its hind legs and crashed to the ground in a swirl of dust.

"Look out, he's kickin'!" somebody yelled.

With a chill of horror, Roy saw a sharp hoof collide directly with Ranny as the injured cowboy hobbled to get out of range of the infuriated animal.

Chapter XV

THE DOUBLE

Cries, mingled with the rush of feet, filled the air as the cowpunchers swarmed over the writhing steer. In a second, Ranny had been snatched away and Mr. Manley was bending over him.

"I—I'm all right," said the young cowboy, trying to force a grin despite his pain.

"Kicked you in the knee, didn't he?" The ranch owner felt the joint, which was already beginning to swell. "Well, I'm glad it wasn't any worse. Carry him to the bunk-house."

While he and Roy went to bandage the limb, Bartlett and Teddy regarded a battered object on the ground.

"Well, it was a good camera once upon a time," the producer said sadly. "Of course, nobody's to blame. When everyone started running to see what had happened, the camera just naturally got itself trampled on."

"That's all right, Chief, we've plenty of spare parts on hand right now. I'll have it fixed in no time at all," promised Harry the cameraman.

"Better get started, old boy, we're pretty far behind on this picture," stated Mr. Bartlett.

When Bardwell Manley came from his first-aid work, he asked the producer to step into his study. "You boys too," he added to Roy and Teddy. After motioning them all to seats, he said, "Bartlett, I hate to throw cold water over things, but——"

"I know, Manley. It's round-up time and you need

all your men on their regular jobs. We've interfered enough as it is." The man's voice was one of mingled sympathy and despair. "In fact, we've brought you nothing but trouble."

The boys' father straightened in his swivel chair. "Hold on, Bartlett, things aren't as bad as all that. We're interested in the picture and mighty grateful to you for making it here. The only thing is, with young Billy gone there's no way of knowing how long——"

"I've been thinking about that," replied the visitor. "Billy's absence is holding up your ranch work. What's more, it's costing my studio thousands of dollars keeping the rest of the cast idle. Tell you what we'll do."

The boys looked at Bartlett questioningly.

"I'll send for Billy's stand-in, a youngster named Carl Ott, who is as nearly a perfect double of him as you'll ever see."

The producer took out a small note-book, withdrew a page and jotted down something.

"Here's a wire I'll send right away. Carl can fly to Denver and take a train to Eagles. He should be here day after to-morrow."

Roy and Teddy volunteered to take the message to Eagles. When they returned from their errand just before supper-time their father and Bartlett were still in the former's study.

"Hello, boys, back so soon?" greeted Mr. Manley. "Mr. Bartlett and I were talking about Billy, wondering whether the Wilsons might have heard anything of him. Sorry I didn't have you wire them while you were there."

Roy smiled. "I beat you to it, Dad. They left their

address with the hotel and I telegraphed them. Here's the answer." He held out a sheet of paper containing a typed message: HAVE HEARD NO WORD ANXIOUSLY WAITING SIGNED WILSON.

Bartlett rose from his chair. "What I can't figure out is why, if Billy really was kidnapped, nobody has been asked for a ransom."

The group sat silent, each occupied with his own thoughts on the subject.

"Well," said the producer at length, "there's plenty to be done on the picture while we're waiting for Ott. Want to help, boys?"

The brothers were more than glad to be busy again. Miraculously the cameraman had repaired the damaged instrument so that it was as good as before. The next two days the filming went on almost incessantly. Visitors to X Bar X were not told of Billy's kidnapping, and the ranch hands were warned to keep the mysterious affair as secret as possible.

Early the morning of the third day Rad Sell rapped on the front door of the ranch-house and was admitted by Roy.

"Just come from town," he said. "Here's a wire."

The message turned out to be from Bartlett's studio, stating that Carl Ott would arrive in Eagles on the afternoon train.

"Shall we meet him for you, Mr. Bartlett?" Teddy asked eagerly.

"Sure thing, boys. Be careful so nobody steals him on the way!"

The producer whispered a few instructions and the brothers departed in the automobile shortly after the noon dinner.

"Carl doesn't know it, but he has more acting to do than he thinks," Roy remarked.

"I'll say! So far as the visitors are concerned, he's Billy Dixon. He'll have to know all the right answers."

Impatiently, the boys settled down in the ramshackle old station to await the train. At length a puff of smoke could be seen on the horizon.

"Golly, the thing's early, Roy, it's only an hour late," Teddy said with a wry grin.

Ten minutes later the train lumbered to a stop and a lone passenger stepped off. Roy caught his breath.

"If I didn't know the secret, I'd bet a million dollars he was Billy Dixon."

"Gives a fellow a funny feeling, all right. Hello, there. Are you Carl Ott?"

The smartly dressed youngster who had disembarked came toward them, carrying a large suit-case. "Hello, fellows," he greeted. "Yes, I'm Carl Ott. Are you from the—the something or other ranch?"

"X Bar X," smiled Roy. "Give me your bag. Have a nice trip?"

"Terrible. They must have built this railway over shell-holes."

Teddy laughed aloud. The newcomer already gave promise of being extremely likeable.

"Well, now, suppose you fellows tell me what this is all about," the young lad remarked as they all headed toward the ranch.

Roy outlined the situation according to Bartlett's instructions.

"If people should find out about Billy's kidnapping, it'll be twice as hard to trace him, Carl," the older Manley explained. "So, if anybody asks you questions, remember you're Billy Dixon and live with the Wilsons in Hollywood."

"You can count on me," Carl declared. "I'm certainly sorry to hear about Billy, though. He and I were good friends."

Early the next morning Bartlett assembled the cast and ordered work to begin immediately.

"We'll take the dancing scenes first, everybody," he announced. "All right, Carl, let's go."

The lot, as usual, was crowded with spectators, many from miles away, who had come early to obtain a good view of the proceedings. The young star took his place before the cameras and commenced a tap dance. Faster and faster he went until the crowd roared with delight.

"Look at that, men!" squealed an old puncher, jumping up and down in a poor imitation of Carl's act.

"Set down, Jed, you ain't got the build fer that," chided another cowboy, whereupon the onlookers burst into laughter.

At length, when Bartlett ordered a rest period for Carl, a round of applause went up for the youngster.

"Lad, where'd you larn all that?" croaked the elderly puncher who had attempted the imitation. The boy smiled innocently.

"Oh, out in Hollywood."

Suddenly a brisk, well-dressed young man stepped from the crowd. "May I speak to you a minute, Mr. Dixon? I'm from a Denver newspaper."

"Surely. What can I do for you?" Carl, panting slightly from the exertion of his dance, leaned against a post near by.

"I just wanted to get a few facts for an article, Billy,"

the reporter said, whipping out pad and pencil. "Now, you live in Hollywood, of course?"

"Yes."

"With whom, may I ask? Your folks?"

"Of course. With Dad and M—I mean, with Mr. and Mrs. Wilson."

"Who are they?"

"Oh, they're relatives."

"What's that?" The reporter threw a sharp look at the young substitute star.

"I said with Mr. and Mrs. Wilson. They're relatives."

The young man scribbled hastily. "Now, it's been rumoured that you were kidnapped. Is that right?"

The crowd pressed close and all ears were on the alert. Carl never batted an eyelash.

"Of course I was kidnapped. Mr. Bartlett took me away to help make this picture."

The reporter turned a deep shade of scarlet as laughter broke out. "That'll be enough. Thank you," he said crisply. Pocketing his pencil, he hurried off, followed by the snickers of the cowboys. Not all of them had understood the significance of the incident, but they had enjoyed the youngster's cool replies.

When work on the picture halted at dusk, supper was ready at the big ranch-house table. An hour later, when the meal was over, Roy suddenly noticed that Carl was nowhere to be seen.

"He was in the living-room a little while ago," Bartlett declared uneasily. "Don't tell me——"

The front door suddenly burst open and Carl, big-eyed with alarm, rushed in.

"Somebody come out quick!"

"What's the matter?" Roy and Teddy exclaimed

together. Bartlett and Mr. Manley hurried from the latter's study.

"Well—I—I—the horses! They're all running away!"

"Horses? Running away?" Mr. Manley looked at the youngster wonderingly.

"I was out looking at them and I must have left the corral gate open. I went over to the bunk-house and all of a sudden——"

A wild neighing filled the air outside and hoof-beats thudded on the turf.

"Come on, Roy!"

Teddy shot out the door with his brother at his heels. Sure enough, the corral gate was swinging aimlessly and the dark shapes of galloping horses could be seen in every direction.

"Star and Flash won't run, Roy. Let's get them!"

As they had expected, their own horses were standing peacefully near the ranch-house porch. Just then Nick Looker rode up.

"Come on, boys, some of 'em has got a pretty good head start over thataway!" he called, pointing with his lariat.

The brothers jumped on Star and Flash and raced after the cowboy.

"Kinda hard t' see, ain't it?" he yelled back. At the same instant he swung his lasso at a fast-moving blotch directly ahead. The shadow kept right on going. "Missed 'im!" he cried.

Roy broke out ahead of the others. An instant later he hurled his lariat, and the flying form stopped with a jerk.

"Nice work!" squealed Nick, galloping up with Teddy to the spot where Roy already was examining the captive animal with his flashlight. The older Manley boy was staring as if he had seen a ghost.

"Nick! Teddy! Isn't this Scout?"

The cowboy took one look at the horse and clucked his tongue. "Jumpin' coyotes, it shore is. That's the mare Billy Dixon was on, 'cause I saddled 'im myself."

The three stared at one another in the weird rays of the flashlight.

Chapter XVI

COWBOYS AND CAMERAS

Suddenly, without warning, the captive horse bolted. Before Roy could collect his wits the lariat, which he had wrapped around his wrist, tightened with a snap and he found himself slithering through the dust at a terrific rate.

Nick and Teddy were frantic. Both jumped on their horses and raced off in the direction the other animal had taken, but the darkness had swallowed it up.

"Wait a minute, Nick, listen!" Teddy yelled, reining in Flash. As the cowboy halted, there came a crackling sound in the underbrush not far ahead.

"He's down by the river, Ted!" Nick yelled.

With a chill of alarm the younger Manley spurred his horse. Nick raced after him. In a moment they came to the bank of Rocky Creek, a tumultuous stream widely known for the number of lives it had claimed among cowboys who were foolish enough to try to swim in it.

"Help!" came a cry from the blackness, faintly audible above the rush of the waters.

Teddy's flashlight stabbed the gloom.

"There he is, hangin' on that rock out'n the middle," Nick gasped, pointing. "Hold on, Roy, we're a-comin' out!"

One look at the torrential current told them that it would be folly to attempt to reach Roy unaided.

"Tell you what, Nick, we'll rope a tree up above.

Then we'll be able to haul ourselves back without much trouble."

"Good idea, Ted, but somebody'd better stay ashore and help pull. You wait here. I'll go out after your brother."

"No you won't, Nick," Teddy objected. "He's my brother, so it's up to me to get him out."

Reluctantly the cowboy gave in. Making his way several hundred yards upstream along the slippery bank, he fastened the end of his lariat to a large tree-trunk.

"All right, here's the coil," he called. "Better tie the other end around your wrist."

A moment later Teddy plunged into the raging current and swam desperately toward the middle. At the same time he felt the water carrying him down-stream with increasing speed. Unless he could reach a point opposite Roy before the current should sweep him past his older brother—Teddy suppressed the thought and swam more desperately than ever.

"Can you still see 'im?"

Nick, on the shore, was shining his flashlight over each of the lads in turn. The cowboy was nearly beside himself with helpless excitement as he watched Teddy battle the fierce waters.

A whitish object loomed up ahead of the swimmer. With a superhuman lunge he caught hold of it as the current tore at him.

"Hurray, you made it!" Nick yelped with joy. "Lemme know when you're ready, Ted."

Clinging to the rock beside his brother, the swimmer waited a moment to catch his breath.

"You ought to be in the Olympic team," Roy gurgled.

The older boy was quivering with the cold and one arm dangled loosely in the water.

"Broken?" Teddy queried.

"Don't know. It's numb, and I can't seem to move it. That's why I didn't try to swim to shore."

After passing the end of the lariat around his brother and himself, Teddy knotted it securely. "Ready, Roy? I'll hold you up while we're pulled in. Ready, Nick?"

At the cowboy's answering shout the brothers let go the rock and slid into the swift current. Bit by bit they watched the dim shore approach.

"Won't be long now, fellows," panted Nick in the darkness.

Nevertheless, it was slow, tedious work, and all three were exhausted when Teddy's feet suddenly touched bottom. A moment later the boys sank to the moist ground, panting heavily.

"Let's see your arm, Roy," said his brother.

A deep circular gash near the wrist indicated where the lariat had been.

"It's beginning to feel easier already, fellows. I should have known better than to wrap a lasso around my arm with a scared horse at the other end."

Nick grunted. "Long as you're alive, that's the main thing. Question now is, where's the hoss, and how'd you get out there in them rapids without yore bathin' suit?"

Roy chuckled. "Your jokes are terrible, Nick. Well, I don't know exactly how I did get in the water, it all happened so fast. I think the pony swerved around suddenly. Something snapped—the rope, I guess—and I went flying."

Nick jumped to his feet. "You boys go on back to the ranch. I'll look around a bit fer the pony. See you later."

Agreeing that a change to dry clothes would be a good idea, the brothers started back immediately.

"Where in the name o' time you two been?" Pop Burns queried as the boys, dripping wet, reached X Bar X some time later.

"Out for a moonlight swim," Teddy grinned. "Is Dad around? Did you get all the horses?"

"Shore did. Here's yore Dad, now."

"Hello, boys, what's happened?" their father asked. "Come on around back. Bartlett and I were fussing with the cameras before to-morrow's work."

Bartlett was working behind the bunk-house in the glare of a searchlight. "Well, you two look like a couple of drowned rats," he smiled. "Better be careful, I can't have my picture stars catching cold."

"We have some news for you," Roy said. "We found Billy's horse."

The producer's jaw dropped. "Not really?"

Excitedly, the brothers related what had happened. Just as they finished, Nick Looker rode up with Scout in tow.

"Thar she be, Mr. Manley, saddle'n all. Shore had a job catchin' 'er the second time."

Excitement soon gave way to more apprehension than ever.

"I kinda wish we hadn't found 'er," Nick went on dismally. "Makes the mystery worser'n ever."

After a renewed discussion of Billy's strange disappearance the boys turned in, planning to be up early the next morning for work on the picture. At the crack of dawn they found the ranch buzzing with activity which centred around a strange-looking structure half a mile away.

"Looks like a fort," Teddy observed. "How'd it get built so fast?"

Bartlett laughed. "You'd be surprised how fast we build things for the movies, my boy. Incidentally, it *is* a fort." He gazed around at the crowd of stars, extras and technicians. "Everybody ready for the dynamite sequence?"

"All set, Chief," barked Harry the cameraman.

At a signal from Bartlett the whole company moved in wagons and on horseback to the new location. The producer cleared his throat.

"All right, has everybody a script? White Feather, where are you?"

"White Feather ready," came the reply as the Indian stepped up.

"Fine. You sneak over to the fort and make believe you're spying through a crack in the wall. Then gallop off." The producer turned to Joel Seabury, the villain in the picture. "You're inside the fort, see? Set the dynamite machine and run out, just the way we rehearsed it yesterday. Only don't get yourself blown up. All right, Harry, shoot!"

A loud buzz announced that the cameras were grinding. White Feather, in full regalia as usual, stole up to the wall of the mock fortress and peered through. A moment later he sprang back on his white horse and charged forward.

"Cut!" Bartlett exclaimed. "Everybody back now, till the explosion's over. Shoot!"

A tense moment passed, then Seabury burst out of

the fortress gateway and ran toward them for all he was worth. Reaching Bartlett's side, he stopped. The silence was broken only by the b-r-r-r-r of the cameras.

"That's very funny," Seabury remarked. "What's the matter with the dynamite?"

"Must have been wet," one of the technicians suggested.

"No, it wasn't wet. I think I forgot to take the catch off the timer. Wait, I'll have a look."

Amid a chorus of warnings Seabury ran inside the fort.

"Come back here, man!" Bartlett yelled frantically. "Hey there, you———"

Bang!

The whole prairie seemed to rock. Stones and debris flew through the air and rained down over the horror-stricken onlookers. In the midst of the confusion a figure darted to the ruined structure and vanished behind one of its jagged walls.

"It's Roy!" screamed Nora, who had been among the spectators.

A dozen cowboys hesitantly started for the spot.

"It's no use," yelled one hoarsely. "He shore can't live through that."

"Look out, the wall's collapsin'!" shrieked another.

As an ominous rumble was heard, the whole group backed away. The towering remnants of the wall quivered and began to topple.

"There he is! He's comin' out!" came a sudden cry from Pop Burns.

A breathless silence swept over the crowd for one tense instant as a figure struggled to extricate itself from the smoking debris.

"He can't get loose! Oh, why doesn't somebody help him?" Nora squealed frantically.

"He's loose, and he's holdin' something! He's got Seabury!"

This time it was Nick who uttered the cry of joy. The cowboy literally flew over the scant two hundred yards to the wreckage.

"Thank goodness, it's you!" he said, upon reaching Roy's side. "Here, let me give ye a hand."

Together they dragged the silent figure of Seabury to safety, and not an instant too soon. With a terrific crash the wall hit the ground behind them, splintering into a thousand fragments. A mighty cheer went up from the awed crowd.

"We'll take Seabury to Doctor Gray at once," ordered Mr. Manley. "Rad, get the car."

The entire company now turned to shower congratulations on the older Manley boy for his heroism.

"You don't know the half of it," Bartlett yelped, his ruddy cheeks aglow. "We took pictures of the whole thing! It'll be the most thrilling rescue ever shown in the movies!"

"Can you really use that in the picture, Mr. Bartlett?" Teddy queried. "Will it fit into the story?"

"Fit? Will it fit?" The producer was beside himself with excitement. "We'll make it fit, boy! It's a knockout."

From a clump of sagebrush not far distant peered a face. A cruel smile spread over its pinched features.

"Too bad the whole outfit didn't blow to Kingdom Come," the person said in a harsh mutter, as his glittering, beady eyes shifted to and fro over the scene.

Roy handed a tin drinking cup back to Pop Burns. "Thanks, Pop. Golly, that tasted good."

"Feel all right?" Bartlett inquired. "Think you can do a few minutes' riding?"

"Mr. Bartlett wants us to be in a scene together," young Carl Ott exclaimed.

The face in the bushes bore a look of astonishment. "My kid!" the voice rasped. "My kid Billy! They must o' got 'im back somehow." Again a smile snaked over the thin lips. "Now's my chance!"

Chapter XVII

A PRISONER ESCAPES

Two dusky hands suddenly descended in a wide arc and met with a sickening slap around the scrawny neck half hidden in the sagebrush. The evil-looking individual who had been peering out a moment before struggled desperately.

"Let go! Let go of me!"

The cry, all but completely stifled, attracted no attention whatever in the group of movie workers and cowboys a few hundred feet away. The vice-like hands loosened. One of them deftly caught hold of the captive's single wrist.

"You One-Arm Kosty?" chanted a heavy voice.

"All right, s'posin' I am?" came the surly reply. "What business is that o' your'n, Indian?"

"Me White Feather. You know me?"

The Indian's expression was mask-like. He did not loosen his tight grip on Kosty. "White man know White Feather?"

"I never heard o'—yes, I know ye!" The caretaker's whine changed to a shrill squeal of pain. "I know ye."

"White man prisoner. Must come with White Feather."

Kosty blinked wretchedly. "What fer?"

"White man kill John Talmadge, no? Must come for trial by tribe of White Feather. Prisoner will pay great penalty, maybe on Hunting Ground."

135

He stared at Kosty, who squirmed. Before the ruffian could reply, the chief had whisked him astride a white mare lingering near by. Lightly the Indian jumped on behind, still holding his victim in a grip of steel. The horse picked its way down the rough trail.

"Good idea of yours, Teddy," Roy was saying to his brother in a low voice. "I've been wondering where White Feather goes on these mysterious disappearances of his."

"Now's as good a time as any to find out. I saw him leave the set and head through the sagebrush. Hello, here's a trail."

Flash had stepped on to a rough path leading from the thicket. At once Roy reined in Star and the boys gazed around.

"If he went this direction he must have taken the trail," Roy commented. "Let's go a little way. Maybe we'll see something."

Fifteen minutes later the brothers halted by a small creek beside the path. Suddenly Roy stiffened in the very act of dismounting.

"Listen!" he whispered.

A sing-song voice sounded through a clump of cottonwood trees. Presently it was joined by a second, which was harsh.

"Sounds like Kosty," Teddy muttered tensely.

"And White Feather," his brother amended. "Let's have a look."

Creeping stealthily through the thicket, the boys perceived the huge figure of the chieftain. He was watering his horse at the same creek which the Manleys had come upon previously. Close beside the Indian stood One-Arm Kosty. It was a moment or so before the brothers realised the latter was a prisoner.

"How long you gonna water that mustang? If I got to go to your tribe, let's have it over with."

"White Feather in no hurry. One-Arm will pay penalty for murder of John Talmadge soon enough."

Roy looked at his brother. Teddy puckered his brow, then swung his gaze back toward the speakers.

"I didn't kill nobody named Talmadge or nobody else, Injun," squawked the caretaker. "Why don't you go back to your movin' pictures? You're a pretty good actor, I been hearin'."

For the first time since they had known the big Indian the brothers saw the flicker of a smile on White Feather's bronze features. For a split second his grip loosened on his prisoner's wrist.

"There, you Redskin!"

Kosty's sharp-toed boot shot out with the speed of a bullet and caught the Indian squarely in the pit of the stomach. As White Feather collapsed One-Arm darted into the dense thicket.

"Take care of the chief; I'll get Kosty," called Teddy.

Leaping from his hiding-place, he rushed after the fast-disappearing caretaker, while his brother hastened to the Indian's side. The man lay doubled up on the ground.

"Steady, White Feather, I'll get some water from the creek." Roy removed his bandanna, soaked it in the stream, and soon had the man feeling better.

"White Feather grateful. Must go now. Catch white man Kosty." He struggled to rise, but Roy held him back.

"Teddy's after him now, White Feather. Just take it easy and rest. If I know my brother, he'll be back with that rascal in no time."

The younger lad was having more trouble than he had bargained for. The ugly caretaker was brandishing a long-barrelled revolver as the two stood panting in a small clearing some five hundred yards distant.

"I'll teach you to run after me," One-Arm was snarling. "Stay where y' are or I'll blow you sky high."

Teddy inched forward. The ruffian was only a few feet away.

"Stand still, I said!"

"Better put down that water-pistol, Kosty. We'll get you sooner or later, anyhow."

The caretaker glared. "You think so? Well, maybe you're not as smart as you think. One more move out'n you and——"

Teddy dived at the leering fellow. At the same instant there was a thunderous report and the younger Manley lad collapsed on the ground, dazed. The next thing he knew, Roy was bending over him.

"Ted! Did he shoot you? Teddy!"

"I—I'm all right, I think." He shook his head vigorously and gradually his blurred eyes cleared.

"There's blood on your forehead. Let's have a look." Roy wiped off the wound with his bandanna. "Boy, that was a close one!"

"Am I—am I really shot?" Teddy smiled wanly.

"Just a little skin sheared off, but if you ask me, that's plenty. Can you walk?"

The boy pulled himself to his feet. "Surely. I'm all right now. I guess I lost my man."

"Shucks, don't worry, we'll catch him later. Come on, let's go back to the ranch."

Rejoining White Feather at the creek, the brothers headed homeward. Both boys were eager to question the Indian further concerning the mysterious John Talmadge. White Feather, however, showed no inclination to speak, so they decided to wait until later.

Bartlett it was who first caught sight of them as they rode through the front gate. "Come on, boys, you're just in time. We're shooting an interior, taking an inside picture," he called.

With only a moment taken to dress the slight abrasion caused by Kosty's bullet, Teddy joined the others. They were jammed in the living-room in the midst of cameras, Kleig lights, and other items of equipment.

"Hurt yourself, Ted?" Bartlett inquired absently. "Never mind, give Harry a hand with the cameras. Roy, you can help me. Everybody ready?"

Miss Warren stood in a corner attired in an apron, and giggling foolishly. "This is the first time anybody ever thought I could cook," she laughed.

"I know you can't cook," Bartlett chuckled, "but at least I hope you'll give the impression you can for the picture."

A roar of laughter followed, but the producer held up his hand for silence. "All right, Harry, get ready to grind. Miss Warren walks to the kitchen, mixes some batter, and cooks a round of flapjacks. While she's doing it a message is shoved under the kitchen door providing a clue to our mystery. Ready, everybody?"

The powerful lights snapped on and the cameras began to buzz. Miss Warren tripped lightly into the kitchen and a few moments later an aroma of baking pancakes filled the air.

"Oh, they're burning," whispered Norine, who had been enjoying the prospect of watching the actress make flapjacks.

"Stay where you are," warned Bartlett in a hushed tone as the girl started for the kitchen. "Let 'em burn!"

Roy, following the producer's instructions, slipped outside and passed a sheet of folded paper under the kitchen door. Miss Warren stooped to pick it up.

"All right, cut," ordered Bartlett. "That's enough for this scene. Now you all can have big servings of Miss Warren's delicious food."

Nora and her mother squealed with laughter, in which the others promptly joined as it became evident the pancakes had been burned beyond hope of being eaten.

Work on the picture progressed rapidly during the next two days, the boys taking an active part in many of the scenes. Bartlett was highly elated as he and the brothers sat discussing the film one evening in Mr. Manley's study.

"We'll be finished in a week at the most," the producer was saying. "If the 'Sagebrush Mystery' isn't the best picture of its kind ever filmed, then I miss my guess."

Out in the kitchen Nora and Norine were busy clearing up. The older woman happened to notice a piece of folded paper lying on the floor near the outside door.

"Sure, and I don't see why people are so careless," she complained. "When they want to throw away somethin', why don't they put it in the scuttle?"

With that she tossed the paper into the fire along

with some other scraps from a bucket by the stove. Her action was to cause a great scare among members of the Manley family as well as to Mr. Bartlett, for the folded sheet had not been intended for the waste basket. It had been slipped under the door by a crafty hand and contained the scrawling message:

"Leave $10,000 ransom for Billy Dixon at cross of rocks by Smoky Creek."

Chapter XVIII

OFF FOR SMOKY CREEK

"We've just about finished the picture work here," beamed Mr. Bartlett one morning, when he met Roy and Teddy. "Fact is, I thought we'd go out now and have the carpenters fix up your bunk-house."

"Any time you're ready," they replied together. "Can we help you?"

Since most of the company's carpenters were needed on the set, the man was glad of their offer. For the next two days they were kept busy. Toward evening of the second day, as they were completing the task, Roy heard a crash in the next room.

"What's that, Ted?" he called.

"Just an old coffee can. Had to knock it out of my way to get this nail in. Say, come here a minute!"

The battered tin was lying on the floor of the sleeping quarters with its lid several feet away. Near by was a wad of dark, rolled-up papers.

"Money!" Roy Manley gasped. "Golly, look at it! Twenties, fifties, hundreds!"

Teddy eyed the bills in astonishment. Suddenly he laughed. "I know, Roy, they're Sing Lung's."

"I'll tell a maverick you're right. SING LUNG!"

A round, impassive face appeared at the entrance to the bunk-house kitchen.

"Bossee Loy call?"

"Come here, Sing Lung. Did you ever find that tlousand dollas. Someblody stolee."

The Chinaman blinked innocently. "No findee tlousand dollas. Someblody stolee."

Roy held out the coffee tin in one hand and the money in the other. "Ever see these?"

Sing Lung gulped. "Oh, vellee solly cause tlouble. Usee coffee box for bank, then forget have put tlousand dollas inside. Muchee thanks."

Beaming with gratitude, the Chinaman hobbled off, clutching the money and muttering excitedly to himself.

"He'll never live that down, Ted. Wait till the cowboys hear about it," Roy laughed.

"I'll say! Well, you about through? I'm ready for a little sleep."

"I'm done. There's a light in Dad's study. Let's see what's doing."

Bartlett and their father were talking together earnestly when the boys entered.

"Any news, Dad?" Roy asked.

"Plenty. Look at this."

He handed a sheet of soiled paper to the boys. Roy read aloud a crudely written message:

"'Bring ransom money to Smoky Creek midnight Saturday or the kid will die. THIS IS YOUR LAST WARNING. WE WILL WAIT NO LONGER.'"

There was an interval of tense silence, then Teddy spoke. "Golly, Smoky Creek is about two hundred miles from here. Out on the desert, isn't it?"

Roy nodded. "I'll get a map."

In a moment he was back. "Here it is, Dad. It's not far from the Indian Reservation."

"So I see," nodded the ranch owner. "Well, Mr. Bartlett and I have been talking it over. We're going to send the money right away, marked."

"Who's going to take it, Dad? May Teddy and I?"

"Well——" The ranch owner hesitated, frowning.

"I tell you what, Dad," Teddy burst out. "We'll take White Feather along. He knows the country down there. Please, Dad, we'll be able to take care of ourselves."

Their father agreed and the brothers hastened to pack. Roy, who completed the task first, sat down to study the map.

"We'll take the midnight train from Eagles to Mound City, Ted. I guess we'll have to hire some camels or something."

"We'll hire 'em. How much time have we?"

Roy glanced at his watch. "Not any too much. I'll go down and see if White Feather is ready."

Mr. Manley and Mr. Bartlett drove the boys to the station. The lads' father gave them last-minute instructions. Reaching into his pocket, he withdrew a bulky package.

"Here's the money, Roy, all marked. Don't lose it, whatever you do. Good luck!"

"Good luck, fellows," Bartlett echoed.

The dimly-lighted two-car train chugged up a few minutes later. The boys boarded it with their impassive companion White Feather.

"Golly, I think I'll not be able to do much sleeping to-night," Teddy remarked as the train jolted onward. "It's just as Carl said, this track must be laid over shell-holes."

"Maybe White Feather will tell us about John

Talmadge," Roy suggested. "Will you?" he asked, turning to the Indian.

At first the chief maintained a grave silence, but under the boy's continued urging he began to speak.

"White man Talmadge good man. Come to my tribe Calicut, say he will help us get money for oil wells dug on Reservation. Seem like fine fellow, but has other white man working for him."

"Who was that, White Feather?" Roy asked.

The Indian was silent for a moment. "White man Kosty," he muttered, scowling.

The brothers eyed each other significantly.

"Talmadge go Washington, get government help," the native continued gravely. "Leave Kosty on Reservation to be representative for tribe. Drink and gamble. Fight with Indians. Ugh!"

"What happened then?" Teddy pressed.

"Talmadge squaw die in Washington. He come back to Reservation with baby and nurse. My tribe angry with him because he employ Kosty. Then Talmadge find out Kosty get big money from stealing."

Roy looked surprised. "Stealing?"

"Indians supposed get government allowance. Kosty forge Indians' names on cheques, present at banks and get money. Talmadge find out, start big fight with Kosty. Indians hear noise, run to help Talmadge."

The boys listened intently above the rumble of the train. "What then?" Teddy queried.

"Big riot. Kosty have arm crushed and Talmadge hurt bad. Posse come, but first White Feather rush away with Talmadge baby and nurse and hide them in village."

"Didn't the police lock up Kosty?" Roy wondered.

"Kosty bad hurt, must go hospital. Medicine man take off arm, but in few days Kosty escaped before police come. Indians punished by government for riot, all fault of Kosty. Ugh!"

The Indian sat silent for a moment, then continued, "Me work to fix affairs of tribe, then leave to find Kosty. People say he kill Talmadge. White Feather look all over West for Kosty."

"Is that how you happened to come to our ranch?" Roy inquired.

White Feather nodded. "Come for Kosty, not movie picture. Find him, catch, then lose him. Some day——" He lapsed into silence again as the train chugged through the darkness.

Roy had a sudden thought. "White Feather, what about Talmadge's baby? Whatever happened to him?"

The Indian stared at the boys a moment, then leaned forward and tapped Roy on the knee. "Baby grow to be—*Billy Dixon!*"

The X Bar X boys were aghast.

"Then Kosty isn't Billy's father after all? Jumping blazes!" cried Teddy.

Chapter XIX

DEATH ON THE HORIZON

"What's this, a hold-up?" Roy asked, as the train stopped suddenly. Peering through the sooty window, he added, "We're at Mound City already."

Teddy glanced at his watch. "No wonder, it's five o'clock."

Quickly gathering their luggage, the three from X Bar X got off, White Feather stalking silently behind the boys.

"What a place," Roy shivered, gazing around at the deserted one-room shack that served as a station. "Where do you suppose we go from here?"

White Feather grunted. "Come," he said, "I know restaurant."

The Indian led them along a deserted street and turned a corner where a dimly-lighted sign confronted them.

"This Pete's place," chanted White Feather. "Open all night."

"So I see," Roy nodded. "Well, a little hot soup ought to taste good."

A short, swarthy man in a soiled apron was lounging behind the counter. As the newcomers entered, his face broke into a broad smile and he advanced to meet them.

"I'll be blowed if it ain't Chief White Feather himself!"

"How," the Indian returned the greeting solemnly. "Boys, this Pete, my good friend. Pete, this Roy and Teddy Manley from X Bar X ranch."

"X Bar X! Bardwell Manley's outfit? Put 'er there, boys, I've heard o' your outfit many a time."

After an animated conversation during which the boys learned that Pete had worked from time to time on various ranches near their own, the proprietor set about preparing a steaming meal.

"And what brings ye down to these parts, boys? Goin' fishin' out in the desert?"

Roy laughed. "Well, maybe we are at that." He winked at Teddy, who suddenly had an idea.

"Pete, have you ever heard of a big fellow named Callahan? Looks like a prize-fighter."

The proprietor puckered his brow. "Callahan? Let me see. Name sounds famil'ar." He looked up. "I think I know who y' mean. Fellow by that name was in town here 'bout a week ago."

"Are you sure?" Roy pursued, trying not to show his excitement.

"Wal, he weighed nigh on to two hundred and it warn't fat neither. Mean-lookin' waddy. Tried to start a fight over't Kelly's bar and the sheriff had to put 'im up fer the night."

Teddy nodded. "That sounds like him, all right. Wonder what he was doing in town?"

Pete put down three steaming plates of stew on the counter. "Wal, now, seems he was tryin' to sell an old hoss to Joe Kinnery at the harness shop. Joe wouldn't give 'im nothin' fer it, so he left the critter there. Went away right after that. How's the stew?"

"Never tasted better," Teddy declared.

The next ten minutes the boys occupied in eating. At length Roy pushed his plate aside.

"Pete, that was perfect," he praised. "By the way, can we hire any ponies around here?"

The proprietor stroked his grizzled chin. "Wal, now, I got a stableful right out thar behind the shop. Long as I know who y' are you can have your pick."

Though the man's horses obviously had seen better days, the brothers were only too grateful for the opportunity of continuing their journey at once. An hour later, their saddle-bags crammed with extra food and water, the three from X Bar X set out for the desert trail leading to Smoky Creek.

"Will reach place by next sunrise," the Indian said as they came to the outskirts of Mound City. "Trail begin now."

He led them through a thicket to a high promontory. It overlooked a vast stretch of desert reaching across the distant horizon. The air was bracing and the boys were eager for what lay ahead.

"Pete gave us the best clue yet, didn't he?" Teddy remarked as they trotted on at a steady pace.

"He certainly did, Ted, thanks to your bright idea of asking him about Callahan. No doubt now about that fellow being mixed up in the kidnapping."

As the day wore on the sun rapidly grew hotter. The boys found it necessary to stop at frequent intervals to rest.

"Golly, White Feather," Teddy burst out when they halted for lunch, "does it get much warmer than this around here?"

The chieftain grunted. "This cool day. North-west wind. Will change to south by nightfall and to-morrow very hot."

"That's a pleasant prospect," Roy commented with

irony. "The point is, I'm beginning to wonder about Billy."

Teddy frowned over his sandwich. "I was thinking the same thing. He's not used to deserts and the heat may be hard on him."

"Well, all we can do is push along as fast as possible. Come on, let's get started."

White Feather held up his hand. "Cannot ride now, too hot," he said.

No amount of persuasion would make him go on until mid-afternoon. Chafing at the delay, the brothers wandered about restlessly until the Indian finally gave the signal to start again.

"White men fools," he grunted. "Ride in heat of day, go to Happy Hunting Ground with fever when night come."

Teddy laughed sheepishly. "Guess you're right, White Feather. Roy, you and I'd better study up on how to cross deserts without getting sunstroke."

Joking and bantering to relieve the tension, they rode over the monotonous ocean of cactus-covered sand. Several hours after darkness had fallen White Feather called a halt.

"Eat now and sleep," he said, drawing forth a tiny alcohol stove from his saddle-bag. Weary from the long ride, the brothers were only too glad to cook a quick supper and stretch out on their blankets.

Roy had just fallen asleep when he awoke with a start. A scant dozen feet away stood a rangy, black shadow. As he watched, the form came closer and a low growl sounded in the darkness.

Possibilities for quick action raced through his mind. There was little time to lose, for the object was creeping stealthily closer. With a chill, Roy realised that no weapon of any sort lay within reach.

Suddenly there was a spurt of flame and a loud explosion. The shadow collapsed on the sand. Roy sprang to his feet just as White Feather, stretched out on a blanket near by, snapped on a flashlight.

"Wolf," grumbled the Indian nonchalantly, rising slowly, a smoking revolver in one hand.

"What under the sun is going on?" Teddy exclaimed, rubbing his eyes and peering around in alarm. He rushed over to where Roy and White Feather stood inspecting the carcass of a giant prairie wolf.

"White Feather, you ought to get a medal for that," Roy declared. "Golly, I thought we were all going to be mince-pie by morning."

The boys were far too excited to sleep. Four o'clock, the time set for their departure, found them more than ready to resume their journey.

"Will reach place by noon," White Feather estimated. "Ready?"

"All ready," the brothers replied together. Soon they were racing across the desert in the cool, soft light of dawn. Every now and then, when a large jack rabbit would dart across their path, the boys would vary the monotony of the ride by chasing the swift animals.

"I'm afraid we'd have to ride one to catch him," Teddy laughed when a rabbit had far outdistanced him in the twinkling of an eye.

"Say, do I see something ahead?" Roy pulled up his horse and squinted toward the horizon.

"Reservation," announced White Feather. "Fifteen mile."

Excitedly, the boys watched a column of smoke grow larger until they could see also tiny rows of tents etched against the sky.

"Wigwams of my tribe," was the Indian's brief explanation. "Someone will come to meet us soon."

The words were hardly out of his mouth when two horsemen galloped toward them from the distance. As they approached, the boys saw they were Indians in full dress.

"Recognise them yet, White Feather?" Roy queried.

"Yes, they are chiefs. Big one Tommy Crow. Other one Black Hawk."

Ten minutes later the two riders galloped up to them and slid to a stop in the sand. The three Indians began a rapid exchange of conversation in their native tongue. Finally White Feather turned to the boys.

"You are welcome to my tribe. Black Hawk will give us fresh ponies at once."

After saluting the newcomers gravely, the men turned and galloped off ahead. By the time the three travellers reached the wigwam village, spirited ponies were awaiting them. A crowd of children had gathered and were watching them curiously.

"Golly, I feel as if we ought to have some feathers on our heads," Roy laughed. "Everybody except the youngsters has them."

Black Hawk smilingly made a remark to White Feather. The latter listened, then turned to the boys.

"My tribe know why you are on journey. My chiefs say if we are successful you will be honoured. We make you Great White Chiefs in Calicut tribe."

Roy and Teddy beamed with pleasure, and both bowed respectfully to Black Hawk.

"Tell Chief Black Hawk we shall be very grateful, White Feather," Roy said seriously.

The Indian translated the boy's message, then Black Hawk held up the palm of one hand and chanted unintelligibly.

"Chief Black Hawk say blessings of Sun Father go with you. Now we leave."

Quickly the boys transferred their saddle-bags to the fresh ponies. Shortly afterward, with White Feather in the lead, they galloped off over the sand.

Two hours later the Indian reined in his horse. "Will reach end of desert by nightfall," he told the boys. "We stop now, cook lunch, and rest."

The heat was terrific. The brothers did their best to make light of it, despite the fact that each was growing more apprehensive over the fate of Billy in the seething atmosphere.

"Have some bacon and eggs," said Roy, holding the frying-pan over their portable stove and passing it to Ted.

"Thanks. Personally, I don't see why we need a stove out here. Why don't you just dump the eggs on the sand? They'll cook twice as fast."

"You're probably right," his brother remarked dryly. "If you ask me, I'd just as soon drink a quart of this cool tomato juice.

The Indian regarded them silently for a moment. "Paleface boys brave, but know nothing of desert travel."

Roy laughed. "We'll admit it." His face suddenly blanched. "Look!" he cried, pointing over their heads.

Chapter XX

THE LONE HORSEMAN

A towering, funnel-shaped cloud split the distant sky like a huge black dagger.

"Coming right for us!" Teddy yelped.

The X Bar X boys stared breathlessly at the terrifying sight. For the first time since they had known him White Feather showed signs of concern.

"Great Spirit angry. Send cyclone to destroy someone, maybe us. Might be paleface Kosty."

"And perhaps all of us," Roy bit off hastily. "Let's do something in a hurry."

White Feather arose. "Cover horses with saddlerobes. Cover selves with blankets. Nothing else to do."

Roy and Teddy moved like lightning. In a moment the eyes and nostrils of their ponies had been bound securely according to the Indian's instructions, and the boys reached for their own blankets. They squatted on the sand and watched with growing horror as the deadly twister swept toward them.

The rumbling grew louder until the whole desert trembled. With the roar of wind came a hiss of whirling sand.

Choking and gasping for breath, the boys threw themselves flat in a desperate effort to evade the storm. Roy felt a terrific stab of pain in his side as a heavy object hit him, but he dared not move lest the wind rip away his blanket. Dimly he heard the plaintive neighs of the horses above the shrill scream of the twister.

The sand passed through his blanket as if it had been a sieve, stinging him like a million nettles. Struggling against a horrible sensation of suffocation, Roy held his breath until his eyes fairly bulged from their sockets and his head pounded as if it would burst. Then, as quickly as it had come, the cyclone roared away into the distance.

"Roy!"

"Hello, Ted! Are we still alive?" asked the older boy, as the brothers poked out their heads. "Where's White Feather?"

"He's gone!"

"And so's everything else except the horses. Look, the saddle-bags were ripped right off!"

"It's a wonder we weren't too. Here comes somebody."

From the top of a small sand dune a dishevelled figure staggered toward them. A moment later, to their relief, they recognised White Feather. The Indian was badly bruised and there was no sign of his proud head-dress.

"Great Spirit not angry with us. We live," he said, squatting down beside his horse.

"How did you ever get carried off so, White Feather?" Teddy asked in astonishment.

The chieftain shrugged. "Strong wind," was his reply.

The boys begged the man to let them examine his wounds, but he waved them off. "Storm over, we go now," he said, painfully mounting his pony.

Reluctantly Roy and Teddy followed suit. For more than an hour they rode steadily.

As darkness settled down, White Feather said, "End of desert near. Smoky Creek not far."

A lone horseman appeared out of the gloom ahead and slithered to a halt beside the Indian.

"Howdy, strangers! Some blow, eh?" He tipped back his sombrero to mop his face with a large bandanna. Over his breast pocket was pinned a badge.

"Certainly was," Roy replied. "Were you in it?"

"Wal, not in the worst of it, thank my lucky rabbit's foot, here. One o' my rangers says it hit worst over't Smoky Creek way. Ain't a tree standin', he says. Where you bound for, men?"

Roy hesitated an instant. "Oh, we're out on a little hunting trip," he replied.

"We're supposed to meet a couple of other fellows around Smoky Creek," Teddy added, describing Kosty and Callahan. "You haven't seen them by any chance, have you?"

The officer eyed the ground reflectively. "Came acrost a fellow campin' the other day that looked like that big one you mentioned, but I ain't seen no one-armed man."

The brothers thanked the ranger, who appeared to be in a great hurry. "So long, fellows, got to get to Mound City." His horse reared and plunged off into the gathering darkness.

"The clue is still good," said Roy as they started up again.

"Yes. Nothing to do now but find the cross of rocks, whatever that is."

Shortly afterward White Feather led them into a narrow trail passing through a dense forest. Abruptly the Indian halted.

"Smoky Creek about one mile. Smoky River bend in

middle, like horse-shoe. Become very narrow for short distance. That part known as Smoky Creek."

As quickly as he had stopped, White Feather clucked to his pony and trotted on.

"Well, that clears up a lot of things I've been wondering about," Roy remarked.

"Same here," added Teddy. "By the way, where do you suppose the cyclone went? I don't see any blown-down trees."

Hardly had the boy spoken when they came to a gigantic tree-trunk across the trail. White Feather snapped on his light and swung it to and fro, revealing a wide swath of uprooted trees passing deep into the heart of the forest.

"Great Spirit do strange things," he commented simply, dismounting and leading his pony around the end of the jagged trunk. The boys followed, soon realising that further riding would be impossible because of the debris strewn across the path.

"We tie horses here. Go rest of way on foot," the Indian decided.

After twenty minutes of floundering in the thicket they emerged at a small clearing. The gurgle of water could be heard near by.

"Smoky Creek," whispered White Feather. "We look for cross of rocks now."

Tense with excitement, the brothers swung their flashlights to and fro over the clearing. Unfortunately it was partly covered with wreckage.

"We wait until daylight," White Feather suggested after a careful search had failed to reveal anything remotely resembling a cross of rocks. The Indian had hardly spoken when Roy uttered a low exclamation.

His companions hastened to the spot where he was standing near a clump of sagebrush. In the rays of his light were a dozen large stones arranged on the ground in the form of a cross.

"A note," Teddy exclaimed, seizing a muddy sheet of paper all but hidden beneath one of the stones. Quickly he unfolded it and read aloud: "'Bury money under rocks. THEN LEAVE.' Well, what shall we do?" he asked.

"We'll do what it says about the money, but we won't leave," his brother whispered. "How about it?" he asked the Indian.

"Bury money. Then White Feather show you secret camping place."

With his hunting-knife Teddy scooped out a handful of soft earth. Then Roy placed the bills his father had given him, in a tin can.

"Well, here's luck," said the younger Manley, replacing the dirt over the container.

At the Indian's insistence, the brothers remained in their secret camping spot deep within the forest until morning. At dawn they drew lots and Roy won the task of a trip to the clearing to investigate. An hour later he was back.

"Nothing's been touched," he announced, trying to hide his disappointment. "And no Billy, either."

"We wait three days, then remove money and leave note," White Feather counselled them. Impatiently the boys settled down for the ordeal of doing nothing. On the morning of the fourth day the Indian agreed the money should be removed. "Write note. Ask kidnappers which night money must be left."

Ingeniously, Roy wrote out a message by using a

charred stick on a piece of bark which White Feather secured. Late that night Teddy slipped through the woods to deposit the note and retrieve the money-container. After nearly two hours had passed and he did not return, Roy began to pace to and fro.

"I'd better go after my brother. Something may have happened to him."

The chieftain watched his young friend gravely. "Not yet. One boy, maybe danger, two boys, maybe twice danger."

Suddenly there was a crackling sound in the thicket and Teddy stumbled into their tiny clearing, breathless with excitement.

"White Feather! Roy! Follow me! Quick!"

Chapter XXI

A CLUE

Without waiting for the others to reply, Teddy turned and dashed back into the thicket. Roy and White Feather were at his heels. In a few moments the younger Manley stopped.

"Quiet from now on," he whispered. "Keep your lights off."

Stealthily the three crept through the forest to the edge of the clearing where the money had been buried. Roy caught his breath. In the pale moonlight a dozen feet away a heavy-set man, swathed in bandages, was digging.

"Know who he is?" Roy whispered into his brother's ear.

"Looks like Callahan. Wonder what happened to him?"

As the brothers stared at the shadowy figure, the man suddenly collapsed. White Feather, crouching beside the boys, nudged Roy.

"Look around carefully before go out to sick man."

The Manleys waited with senses alert, but there was no sign of anyone else in the vicinity. The Indian nodded.

"We go out now."

Cautiously the group stepped from the brush toward the motionless figure. Teddy snapped on his light.

"Callahan, sure enough!"

Roy hurried to the creek, returning presently with

his bandanna wet. A few moments later, under the skilful ministrations of both boys, the ruffian began to regain consciousness.

"Callahan! Wake up!" Teddy called loudly.

The man's eyes fluttered. Suddenly he raised himself, blinking in the glare of the light.

"Who—where——?" His face was pale and drawn and he obviously was suffering greatly.

"We're the Manleys, Callahan," ventured Roy.

"Oh, yes. Well, I surrender. I ain't goin' to last long now, boys." The fellow's voice had become little more than a feeble gasp.

"We'd better get him to a doctor," Roy decided.

"I guess we'd better. He looks——"

White Feather tapped Teddy on the shoulder. "Ask questions now," he muttered. "If White Man Callahan go to Hunting Ground, questions not answered."

The brothers whispered together for a moment, then Teddy disappeared into the thicket. Roy turned to the sorely stricken cowboy again.

"Where's Billy Dixon, Callahan?" he demanded sternly.

The coarse-looking fellow moaned. "He—he run away from me. He——" A shudder of pain swept through his giant frame. "I was keepin' him over Torture Cave way—campin'. I took good care o' him—honest."

"You haven't any idea where he went?"

"No. He got away last week. I was goin' to—goin' to——" His breathing came in a series of short gasps. "I was goin' to look for 'im now, but I got caught in the blasted twister. I——" He suddenly sank back on the ground, his eyes closing slowly.

Teddy reappeared at that moment leading their horses. "All ready, Roy?"

"I'm afraid it's too late, Ted. We'll try, anyhow."

"White Feather hold paleface on horse," the Indian said. "We go to Pioneer Village, little settlement four mile south."

Together they lifted Callahan's silent form on to White Feather's horse and the Indian mounted, holding him in his arms. After what seemed to Roy and Teddy an eternity of floundering in the dense underbrush, feeble lights flickered in the distance. Then they arrived at the settlement.

"Medicine man friend of White Feather. We go there."

The Indian led them to the door of a modest house in the centre of the village, where they roused the physician.

"He's gone to the Happy Hunting Ground, White Feather," said the doctor when they carried the injured cowboy into his consulting-room. "I'll see to it that he gets a decent burial."

The Indian gravely withdrew a bulky wallet from his pocket and pressed a roll of bills into the physician's hand. "White Feather grateful," he mumbled.

The boys held a hasty conference with the chieftain when they were outside again.

"We must head for Torture Cave," Roy declared. "Billy's surely around there."

"Not necessarily," his brother objected. "I don't see what else we can do at the moment, though."

White Feather agreed to guide them to the cave. "We reach there at sunrise."

Before departing they stopped at the village store and roused the proprietor to get supplies.

"Roy, I think we ought to get in touch with the ranch just as soon as we can. Maybe Billy's back there now," said his brother as they rode along.

"Golly, perhaps you're right. But how are we ever going to get a message? Boy, this hill is steep!"

As they reached the top of a rise in the trail a horseman travelling in the opposite direction nearly collided with White Feather. "P—pardon me, strangers!" he said with a startled glance. "Guess I wasn't lookin' where I was goin'."

"That's quite all right," Roy grinned. "Not much room to pass on this trail."

The newcomer showed no disposition to hurry on. "Where bound, fellows?" he smiled engagingly, adjusting the wrinkled bandanna around his neck. Without waiting for an answer, he continued, "I'm not goin' any place in p'ticular, so maybe you won't mind if I ride along with you f'r a while, eh?"

Roy eyed the pleasant-looking young face doubtfully.

"I'm Slim Batty, just call me Slim. Stubby, my pony, and me are just a couple o' roamin' cowhands lookin' f'r a place to light. And we're not bad company, either."

Despite their impatience at being interrupted, Roy and Teddy could hardly suppress a grin at the irresistible fellow's determination.

"All right, you can ride along with us for a while," Teddy said.

The cowboy fell in beside them. "Oh, don't worry, men, I won't wear out m' welcome. But Stubby'n me likes company, an' when we run into strangers we like to talk to 'em, don't we?" He patted his horse fondly and the brothers winked at each other. White Feather, riding ahead, paid no attention to him.

"If what you say is true, you must get around a lot," Roy remarked. "Ever hear of the X Bar X ranch?"

Slim nodded without a second's hesitation. "Shore thing. Just the other day, in fact. Met a young fellow, couldn't have been more'n twelve y'ars old——"

The boys listened eagerly.

"Wal, he was campin' and I was campin', so we camped together one night on the trail. Said he was a movie actor at X Bar X. Movie actor on a ranch, can ya beat that?" The cowboy burst into laughter. "When he says that, I know he's plumb loco, so Stubby'n me clears out fast as we kin."

The boys were now beside themselves with excitement. Roy struggled to keep his voice calm. "Slim, we're looking for that fellow. Do you know where he is?"

The other stared at them wonderingly. "You're lookin' f'r him? What do you fellows do, run a bug-house?"

"Well, maybe," Teddy smiled. "Anyhow, we're trying to find that youngster. Tell you what, Slim, can you take us to the place where you and he were camping?"

The young cowboy pursed his lips. "Wal, I think I might. How 'bout it, Stubby? 'Course, it won't be easy. Pretty rough country around there." He eyed the Manleys significantly, and they rode on for a moment in silence. "No," said Slim at length, "I don't think it'd be worth it."

Roy suddenly plunged his free hand into his breast pocket and withdrew a roll of bills. Extracting several, he handed them to the cowboy, who smiled broadly.

"Now you're talkin', fellows. Here we go!"

Chapter XXII

STOLEN MONEY

White Feather, who had remained silent throughout their ride thus far, called a halt at noon.

"We camp now. Creek not far off trail. Get water for cooking."

"Good idea," Roy declared. "And thank goodness we're going to have something besides the jack rabbits we've been living on for a week." Reaching into his saddle-bag, he withdrew several cans of vegetables which they had purchased at the settlement.

"Stranger, go get water," White Feather ordered, handing a small bucket to Slim.

The cowboy winced. "Stubby'n me don't like work, y' know. Well, maybe we'll get a little water," he added hastily as the huge chieftain stared at him silently. A moment later he had disappeared into the thicket.

"I can't say as I care much for our new travelling companion," Roy commented in a low tone.

His brother nodded with a frown. "I don't either. Shiftless sort of fellow. Maybe we ought to get rid of him."

The older X Bar X boy shook his head. "No, Ted, we owe it to Billy to put up with anything to find him."

Slim appeared just then with the water-bucket half full. "Here y' are, boys. Couldn't get any more in it without spillin' it."

Ignoring the fellow's half-insolent attitude, the boys

quickly made a fire and soon had lunch prepared. The cowboy ate wolfishly while White Feather sat observing him in sullen silence. At length the Indian rose.

"Time to go," he announced.

"Say, who's runnin' this party, me or that Injun?" whined Slim.

Twenty minutes were wasted while the brothers sought to explain that the chieftain was the leader of their group.

"Well, all right, seein' as you insist." The cowboy rode several miles without speaking. Finally, toward dusk, he broke his self-imposed silence. "Ain't it about time to put up f'r the night, fellows?"

When White Feather shook his head, they rode on farther. At length the Indian halted. "We stay here for night." He pointed to a clearing, and the brothers, exhausted from the day's happenings, soon cooked supper and crawled into their blankets.

At dawn Roy woke up with a start. Gazing around at the sleeping forms, he spied an empty blanket between the figures of the Indian and his brother.

"Ted! White Feather!"

The younger Manley opened his eyes. "What's the matter? Go on back to sleep."

"Slim's gone! So is his horse."

Teddy and White Feather jumped to their feet. At the same moment Roy, plunging his hand into his pocket, turned white as a ghost.

"The money's gone too!" he gasped.

The three looked at one another helplessly. At length White Feather rubbed his chin thoughtfully. "We fools to trust stranger. Nothing to do but go on to Torture Cave, look for Billy there."

Disconsolately, they broke camp and set out with the Indian as their guide. It was slow going, for the trail was gradually leading them into mountainous country.

"Many wild horses here," White Feather remarked as they picked their way carefully up and down the rocky trail. "Maybe see some."

Teddy uttered an exclamation a few moments later as they reached a bluff overlooking a wide plain. "There's a herd now, Roy. See them down there, like tiny specks?"

"I think I spy something else. Isn't somebody running toward them?"

The boys and White Feather watched wonderingly as a small figure broke away from a clump of trees and headed toward the milling herd of mustangs.

"Him paleface we look for!" White Feather's remark dropped like a bombshell and the boys turned to the Indian quickly.

"You mean he's Slim?" Roy queried.

The Indian was gazing in the distance with the eyes of a hawk. "Yes. Him horse run away, join mustangs maybe. We go see."

"Right!" agreed the brothers.

Scrambling down a steep path leading to the valley, they galloped toward the herd at full-tilt.

"Yes, that's our friend Slim, all right," Teddy panted. "How's that for luck?"

The cowboy, his back toward them, apparently did not hear their approach. The thumping of the mustangs' hoofs as they milled about was too loud.

"Rope him, Ted!" Roy called.

His brother whipped out his lariat and twirled the coil over his head. At the same instant Slim spun around, uttered a cry, and took to his heels. A split second before he reached the refuge of a clump of near-by trees the rope slithered through the air, tightened with a jerk, and the fugitive crashed to the ground. In a twinkling the boys were upon him.

"Get off me, I ain't done nothin'," the cowboy whined, squirming under Roy's knee.

"No? What about this?" demanded Teddy, reaching into Slim's pocket and drawing out a wad of bills.

The cowboy laughed sheepishly. "Oh, that? How'd that get there, anyhow?"

"You know well enough how it got there, Slim Batty," Roy said sternly. "I think we'll just turn you over to the rangers."

Slim's face blanched. "Please, fellows, don't do that. I'm sorry I took y'r money, but, well, Stubby'n me ain't had much work lately."

At length the boys took pity on the fellow, and Roy went so far as to locate Stubby in the herd of mustangs. With White Feather's aid he managed to get close enough to the high-strung wild horses to rope and lead back the animal.

"There you are, Slim. Now get out of here before we change our minds and start the rangers after you."

Slim jumped on his horse and waved. "Thanks!" He dug his spurs into Stubby's side. "You half-wits!" he hissed as he raced off into the forest.

"Nice fellow," Teddy remarked dryly. "I'd like to do more for him."

His brother grunted. "So would I, with a whip. Well, let's get going."

"We reach small settlement to-night," White Feather said as they resumed the tedious journey over the trail.

"Then early to-morrow we arrive Torture Cave not far from settlement."

"What do you know about that, Ted, a real bed to-night for a change."

"Suits me," his brother laughed. "I've marks on me from just about every rock and snag for fifty miles around. Do you suppose we'll be able to sleep on a mattress?"

Laughing and joking, they pushed steadily onward, little realising what was taking place at that very moment at a fork in the trail a few miles behind them.

"What's that you say?" a stern-looking horseman in an officer's uniform was demanding. "You met some counterfeiters?"

The pleasant-faced young man in sombrero and chaps nodded. "That's right, Sheriff, warn't more'n an hour ago they got away. Y'see, I meets 'em on the trail, an'——"

The officer waved his arm impatiently. "Never mind no long yarns. Which way'd they go?"

"See this fork in the trail here? That's the one they took. Man alive, wait'll y' ketch 'em and see all the money they got. Y' cain't mistake 'em, Sheriff, two young fellers and an Injun."

"Much obliged. I'll get some o' my men and we'll capture 'em 'fore they know it." Wheeling around, the man galloped off, while Slim smiled unpleasantly to himself. "I guess that'll fix them smart alecks. Come on, Stubby, let's clear out."

A dozen miles away Roy and Teddy were lying on two soft beds in the Wayside Inn at Prairieville.

"By golly, I never knew it could feel so good to lie down and rest," Teddy was declaring fervently.

"Agreed, old boy. Well, we'll have plenty to do to-morrow if we're going to wander around Torture Cave. A little sleep now won't hurt us any."

As the old grandfather's clock at the inn was striking midnight, the brothers were awakened by a loud rap on their door.

Chapter XXIII

THE BEARDED HERMIT

"Open up in the name o' the law!" rang out a booming voice.

The boys sprang from their beds in alarm. Before either of them could reach the door, half a dozen burly men had swarmed into the room.

"Whar's the Injun?" demanded one. "Pete, you an' Joe go look for 'im."

"Say, what's all this about?" Teddy blazed forth, as two of the officers seized him.

"Ye know counterfeitin' ain't allowed, don't ye?" rasped the leader of the group. "Hand over the money."

Roy and Teddy looked at each other dazedly. "Counterfeiting?" the older Manley boy gasped.

"Won't do ye no good to hide nothin', young fellers. Sam, search them clothes."

There was an interval of silence, broken only by the rustle of the boys' garments as a ranger fumbled through the pockets. Suddenly he hesitated, then triumphantly drew forth a large roll of bills.

"That's good," boomed the sheriff. "Just like I thought, too. Hand 'em over, Sam. Lemme take a squint at 'em." He scrutinised the money under the light. "Yep, here's the evidence, men. Look, Jim, see them markin's? What do you think o' that f'r darin'?"

"And them so young, too." The man named Jim eyed the boys with a look of mingled sympathy and disapproval.

"Cain't help that, it's their own fault," snapped the sheriff.

"I tell you——" Roy began, but the officer waved him aside.

"The constable will hear all that, young feller. Better keep yore mouth shut. Wonder what's holdin' Pete and Joe up with that Injun?" He turned to the boys again. "Didn't you two have an Injun with ye?"

Neither of the brothers spoke. Teddy, his face flushed with rage, had all he could do to hold himself in check. Just then footsteps sounded in the corridor and White Feather entered, escorted by two men. The Indian eyed the others coldly.

"So here y' be," thundered the sheriff. "Well, you know what happens to Injuns as gets mixed up with——" He suddenly stared at White Feather as if the latter had been a ghost.

"Ain't I seen him before?" interjected Sam.

"I was just thinkin' the same thing," said the sheriff. "What's yore name, Injun?"

"White Feather. You Sheriff Rogers. Treat old friends very bad."

"Wal, I'll eat a prairie dog!" The officer's weather-beaten face was wreathed in smiles. "Men, you remember White Feather, the Injun that fixed up that mess down't the Reservation when John Talmadge was knifed?"

There was a chorus of exclamations as they crowded around the grave chieftain, shaking his hand and plying him with questions.

"That shore puts things in a different light," the officer declared when the excitement had subsided. "'Course, as a matter o' official routine, we ought to know whar this here money come from. How 'bout it?"

There was nothing for the boys to do but explain the whole situation. To their relief, Sheriff Rogers agreed not to interfere with their plans.

"If White Feather's goin' along with you, then we'll keep our hands off till you say the word, boys. Good luck."

The men trooped out, leaving Roy and Teddy open-mouthed in the middle of the room.

"Well," said the younger Manley at length, "that's two medals for White Feather; one for shooting the wolf and the other for saving us from a lot of trouble with the law."

Roy laughed. "I'll tell a maverick! Golly, we might have been in jail by morning."

As the Indian gravely withdrew to his room, Roy had an idea. "Maybe we can communicate with home, Ted. Do you suppose there's a phone anywhere in the village?"

"There should be," said his brother.

The proprietor of the inn, who had been roused by the commotion, nodded vigorously. "Shore thing, young feller, we have the only phone in the county. Just turn the crank and git the operator, if she ain't asleep."

The boys retired to a musty corner of the dining-room, where an old-time model hung on the wall. After an hour of turning the crank and talking with several operators in turn, Teddy was able to dispatch a tele-gram through a distant railroad depot.

"If luck's on our side we'll have an answer by break-fast-time," said Roy as his brother hung up.

At dawn their bedroom door opened. "Message fer

ye," cackled a voice, as the proprietor hobbled in in his nightshirt, holding out a slip of paper. "Jest come over the phone. I writ it down."

"Roy, wake up. Here's our answer."

"Any news?"

"Listen: '*Kosty made unsuccessful attempt kidnap Carl Ott stop movie finished all leaving except Bartlett stop no sign Billy stop come home soon love Dad.*'"

"In other words, we're still right where we started. Well, let's wake White Feather and go on our way."

After a hasty breakfast the trio started out again. Soon the little village was left behind.

"Coming cave country," said the Indian as the trail took a steep turn and began winding into the heart of a mountain. "Not far go now."

The boys felt their pulses quicken, but Roy's face was grim. "If only we can find a clue around Torture Cave," he sighed.

"I have a hunch something's going to turn up this time," Teddy said confidently. "At least, we know Billy was around here a few days ago."

"He's not in the clutches of that Callahan, anyway."

Just then the Indian halted and cocked an ear toward the ground. "Horse come," he grunted. "White Feather hear rattle of stone."

As they listened intently the sound of hoof-beats was unmistakable. A moment later a grotesque-looking animal bearing a strange figure came toward them over the brow of the hill.

"A mule," Teddy whispered, "with Santa Claus on his back."

"He certainly looks like Santa Claus at that." They watched in wonderment as an old man with a flowing white beard approached on his squat, long-eared mount.

"Good morning, strangers," he greeted them in a calm voice.

"Him hermit," White Feather said. "Him live alone in mountains."

"Good morning, sir," said Roy. "Rough trail, isn't it?"

The recluse smiled. "Not so rough as the trail of life. Whither bound, pray tell?"

"We were going to Torture Cave, Mr.——" Teddy began.

"They call me Father Happy. You are going to Torture Cave? I showed it to Billy only yesterday. Quite a sight for—why, is something wrong?"

The boys were staring, open-mouthed. "Oh, nothing is wrong," Roy laughed. "When you mentioned that name I——"

"You mean Billy? Oh, Billy is my pride and joy. Youngster about twelve. I found him wandering half starved in the woods."

White Feather's usually mask-like face became wreathed in smiles. The brothers were fairly beside themselves with relief.

"Stop! Pray wait a moment," cried the bewildered hermit as Roy and Teddy whooped with joy, wringing the old man's hand and besieging him with questions.

"We have been searching for a kidnapped boy named Billy Dixon," Roy explained.

"That is his name, all right—Billy Dixon," the strange old man exclaimed, promising to take the three wanderers to his place of abode at once. "Billy is out hunting now, but should be back soon."

"Don't worry, sir, we'll be only too glad to wait," Teddy yelped joyfully as they turned into the thicket and began a long, difficult ascent.

"I must apologise for my rude hut," the hermit said, stopping a short while later for a brief rest. "You see, I live very simply and devote most of my time to contemplation."

Bursting with excitement, the boys followed their bearded guide deep within the forest and finally emerged on a narrow plateau, at one end of which was a crudely constructed shelter of logs.

"Here we are, boys. Billy!" He placed two fingers to his mouth and emitted a shrill whistle. "I guess he'll be back soon. Come in, won't you?"

The single room was bare of furnishings save a heavy wooden table and chair and a few cooking utensils lying about. A blaze was crackling merrily in a stone fireplace at one end.

"Make yourselves comfortable, boys," the kindly old man urged.

Roy and Teddy promptly stretched out by the fire while White Feather, as grave and silent as always, remained outside to curry their horses. The day wore on, and almost before they knew it darkness had begun to settle over the quiet hilltop.

Billy had not returned!

Chapter XXIV

LOST IN THE CAVERN

Roy began to pace restlessly over the stone floor of the hermit's hut.

"You must be calm," the old man said gently. "He will return, I am sure."

The fire had burned low. Its glowing embers cast weird shadows through the room. Suddenly Teddy jumped up.

"I'm not going to stand this suspense any longer!" he cried. "I'm going out and look for Billy."

The hermit took the boy by the arm. "It will be of no use now, son. The darkness, the crevices in the rocks, you might fall into one."

The younger Manley lad's voice shook slightly. "I'm sorry, but I just can't stand it any longer."

Roy walked to the doorway and peered out. "Where's White Feather?"

"That's right. I'd forgotten all about him," his brother said. "Isn't he outside?"

"Don't see him. White Feather, are you there?"

"——are you there?" floated back a hollow echo from the distance. Roy shivered. "Where do you suppose he went to?" he demanded irritably.

The extreme tenseness of the situation was beginning to tell on the boys. Teddy's flashlight stabbed the darkness. "His horse is gone, Roy!"

The boys stared at the vacant space beside their ponies. "That settles it, I'm going for certain," declared the younger Manley lad.

"And I'm with you," Roy echoed.

The hermit regarded them for a moment. "Very well, boys, I shall go too. Perhaps I can help, for I know the countryside thoroughly."

For more than two hours the three stumbled over rocky bluffs and along narrow, littered trails, pausing frequently to shout. Each time tantalising echoes sped back through the dismal night air, but no other sounds were heard. At length the hermit persuaded them to return to the hut until daylight.

"I can't understand White Feather's disappearance," Roy muttered.

"Golly, if we can't trust White Feather, whom on earth *can* we trust?" asked Teddy.

Neither lad could sleep that night. The morning sun streaming in through chinks in the walls was a welcome sight. Roy was about to rise from his blanket by the fireplace when the old man hobbled in.

"Boys! The Indian is coming."

The Manleys bounded to their feet as White Feather solemnly stepped through the doorway.

"For goodness' sake, what's happened?" Teddy blinked. "Where is your horse, White Feather?"

"Pony dead."

"Dead!"

"White Feather go out, look for Billy when darkness fall last night. Cut through thicket, suddenly drop through heap big hole in rocks, could not see in dark."

"Dropped through a hole in the rocks?" Roy repeated, unbelieving.

"He must have fallen through a crevice," the hermit said. "There are many of them hereabouts, as I think I told you before."

White Feather continued in his characteristic monotone, "Find self in cave. Horse break fall, but die on
rocky ground. White Feather climb 'round with flashlight for long time, then see stars in sky through crack
and climb out."

The Indian's recital left his listeners wide-eyed. Then
Roy frowned. "Golly, do you suppose the same thing
happened to Billy?"

The old man nodded slowly. "I have been thinking
that. We shall go out at once. I have torches for us all."
He scurried into a corner and brought forth four long,
rod-shaped devices, each with a cup attached to one
end. "Here you are, boys, and here's one for White
Feather." Then he fastened a small gourd to his belt.
"This contains oil. I notice that you have flashlights,
but they may burn out just when we need them
most."

A few moments later, with the hermit leading, the
group set out to explore the vicinity on foot. After an
hour of investigating a number of small caves and
crevices the hermit called a halt.

"I suggest that we split up and meet here at this spot
at noon. White Feather can come with me and you lads
can go on together."

The boys readily agreed that such a plan would
enable them to cover more territory in a vastly shorter
time. Accordingly, the hermit gave each of them a
measure of oil for their torches.

"Be careful, boys. We'll meet you soon."

Waving fondly, for the old man had become attached
to Roy and Teddy and they to him, he turned into a
thicket with White Feather trailing behind.

"Well, which way?" Roy speculated.

"Let's climb up this bluff. Looks as if there might be some caves around."

After they had beaten their way through the dense underbrush for about half a mile, Teddy suddenly caught hold of his brother's sleeve. "Roy! I thought I heard something."

The brothers listened intently.

"Sounds like a voice yelling way off," said Roy.

A strangely muffled cry sounded repeatedly. Then the boy noticed a gaping split between two giant boulders near by. "Ted, is it coming from down there?"

Hurrying to the brink of the yawning crevice, they listened again.

"It's Billy, sure as you're alive," Roy exclaimed. "He's lost!"

Poking their flashlights into the chasm, the boys beheld a huge subterranean cavern lined with fantastic crystal formations of various sizes and shapes.

"Come on, Roy, let's climb down."

Cautiously the lads lowered themselves over the brink and groped their way down the steep, jagged wall to the floor of the cave a hundred feet below.

"Here's a passage, Roy."

A long, irregular corridor stretched out before them in the rays of Teddy's light. At that moment the weird cry sounded again.

"Billy! Where are you?" Roy shouted in reply.

His voice echoed back and forth with a hollow, ringing tone. Suddenly, to their consternation, Teddy's flashlight went out, plunging them into darkness.

"Never mind, mine still works," said Roy confidently. He snapped on the button and a feeble gleam responded.

"Why on earth didn't we bring along some extra batteries?" he groaned.

They stumbled through the passage to a point where several paths branched out. Debating a moment, the boys selected the widest one and proceeded along it to a sharp bend. There was a sudden cry and a figure staggered into the dim rays of Roy's light.

"Billy!" cried both Manley boys.

At the same instant the flashlight flickered out.

Chapter XXV

HOME AT LAST

"Is it really you? Roy and Teddy Manley?" came a feeble gasp.

"It certainly is, Billy," the older Manley lad replied in a voice choked with joy. "Wait a minute till we light these torches. Ted, hand me the matches."

There was an interval of tense silence. "I haven't any, Roy. White Feather took them yesterday."

The situation suddenly became desperate. A single mis-step in the awful blackness might mean a terrible death in one of the many crevices and fissures in the floor of the cave.

"I found a wallet while I was here, fellows," Billy faltered. "Just happened to stumble on to it. Maybe it has some matches inside." The youngster fumbled for a moment. "No, there's nothing in it but a roll of papers."

Roy struggled to keep his voice calm and unconcerned. "Well, let's go back to the fork. I think we can manage to reach that all right."

Holding to one another, with the oldest lad in the lead; the three stumbled through the blackness. Now and then an eerie flutter of wings could be heard.

"Bats," murmured Billy. "I've been hearing them for hours and hours." Teddy could feel the young boy shudder.

Finally Roy stopped. "It's no use," he muttered

"A towering, funnel-shaped cloud split the distant sky"

See page 154

disconsolately. "We must have passed the fork and taken some other passage. We'll just have to——"

"Listen!"

Teddy grasped his brother's shoulder. Not far from them someone was singing a hymn in a ringing bass voice. A sudden light flickered over the walls ahead of them and two familiar figures appeared carrying flaming torches.

"R-e-s-c-u-e the P-e-r-i-s-h-i-n-g," one of the men was chanting. "R-e-s—why, bless the Lord!"

"Father Happy! White Feather!" exclaimed Roy and Teddy together, and a joyful reunion ensued.

"Providence is kind," beamed the hermit. "As White Feather would put it, the Great Spirit guided us to you. But come, let us go back. I fear our young friend here needs warmth and nourishment."

An hour later they were all seated beside a roaring fire in the hermit's cottage, listening to Billy's account of the hardships he had endured after the ruffian Callahan had whisked him away. When the boys related what had happened to the cowboy, Billy's face registered first surprise, then concern.

"I still have my father to fear," he said. "He will be all the more determined to find me now that Callahan is out of his way."

Roy looked at White Feather, who nodded almost imperceptibly. "Billy, I think we have a surprise for you. White Feather is going to tell you."

Wide-eyed with astonishment and joy, the young boy listened as the chieftain related the tale of Talmadge. "White Feather know you are son of Talmadge, not of One-Arm," he concluded solemnly, whereupon Billy jumped up and squeezed the Indian's massive palm.

"That is the most wonderful news I have ever heard, White Feather. Thank you for telling me!"

Excitedly, the visitors discussed plans for departing the next morning, though secretly each was unhappy over the prospect of leaving the kindly old hermit.

Reluctantly, the boys sprawled out on their blankets and tried to compose themselves for sleep. At length, one by one, they dozed off with the exception of Roy, who lay listening to the soft splutter of the dying embers in the fireplace.

Suddenly the lad thought he heard someone moving about in the shadows. Straining his eyes in the gloom, he made out the dim figure of the old hermit stealthily crossing the room toward one corner, where he stopped.

For a moment Roy held his breath. Should he get up and investigate? Perhaps the old man was ill. Before he could reach a decision he heard the faint splash of water in a bucket, followed by a soft *snip snip*.

Teddy leaned over. "What's he doing?" the younger Manley whispered into his brother's ear.

"I can't imagine. Think we should get up and look?"

At that moment the rays of a flashlight pierced the room and White Feather stood up.

"You John Talmadge," he exclaimed more loudly than the boys had ever heard him speak before.

With two strides the Indian crossed the whole length of the room to where a startled man was blinking into the light. As Roy and Teddy jumped up, there came a soft laugh.

"I was going to surprise you. Yes, I am John Talmadge, White Feather."

"Then you're not a hermit after all?" Teddy queried in wonderment.

Talmadge smiled. "I *was*, my boy, but now I have shaved off my whiskers, as you can see. I am going to return to civilisation with my son."

Billy, who had joined the little group gathered around Mr. Talmadge, was speechless with joy. Laughing and crying by turns, he clung to his father until Roy finally persuaded him to rest until morning.

At dawn the entire group was up and ready to leave. Shortly before, Roy and Teddy had returned from a near-by ranger's headquarters with horses for Billy, his father, and White Feather. Two days later, after an uneventful though highly enjoyable journey, they reached the X Bar X ranch.

"By the way, Billy," said Roy when the excitement of their return had subsided and they had finished relating their adventures to the Manley family, "didn't you say you had found a wallet?"

"Gee, I'd forgotten all about it," cried the young movie star. "Here it is." He withdrew a bulky leather pouch from his pocket and handed it to Roy.

"Him Hadley Slater's wallet," White Feather interrupted, peering at the object. "Open, see if money there."

A chorus of exclamations went around the room as Roy brought out a thick roll of bills. The Indian grunted. "That prove him lose life by accident, not murder. If murder, someone would steal money."

A week later, in response to a wire from the Manley boys, Mrs. Slater arrived from New York and was given the wallet.

"I am so thankful," the kindly old lady said with tears in her eyes. "Nothing can bring my husband back to me, of course, but at least I know he died accidentally while he was exploring. That was his favourite pastime. He could not have wished the end to have come any other way."

A few days later White Feather and Ranny, who had in the meantime disappeared, returned with One-Arm Kosty. They had captured the man in a wood after a desperate fight. The surly caretaker was turned over to the police, later confessing that he had cheated the government of thousands of dollars rightfully belonging to White Feather's tribe, and that Talmadge was in no way responsible for what had happened at that time. Kosty admitted, furthermore, that Billy Dixon was Talmadge's son.

"Well," said Mr. Manley one day upon returning from a business trip to Denver, "what do you think I did while I was away?"

Roy smiled. "I hope it was nothing dangerous, Dad."

The ranch owner chuckled. "No, it wasn't dangerous, but just as thrilling. I saw my sons in the movies. I went to a show called——"

"'The Sagebrush Mystery'!" both boys exclaimed together.

"Right you are. And that's only part of it, lads. The other half is the fact that every newspaper in the country is running the story of Billy Dixon and your rescue of the youngster. The result is that more people are flocking to see that movie than ever have gone to see another!"

Shouting with joy, the brothers ran out to tell the news to Billy and Mr. Talmadge, who were staying at the ranch until the boy's next scheduled picture. Both were highly elated, as was Nick Looker, who happened to stroll up to the corral where they were standing.

There was a look of pride in the man's eyes. Another success for the brothers! What would come next? At the moment Nick could not know it would be a strange adventure called "The X Bar X Boys in the Haunted Gully". Now he smiled, laid a hand on a shoulder of each boy, and spoke in praise of their recent work.

"That's mighty fine, lads," drawled the handsome cowboy. He pulled out of his mouth the sliver of straw he was munching. "That don't excuse neither of ye, or you either, Billy, from helpin' in the round-up we started this mornin'. Go git yore chaps on!"